When the last paper was picked up he stood and held out his hand to her.

She took it and stood up too close for comfort. Chest to chest, she looked up into his dark, soulful eyes. Her heart stumbled and every nerve ending in her body tingled. Suddenly the high school crush she remembered from so long ago was standing right here in front of her. All she had to do was reach out and touch him. She licked her lips. An instant later she grabbed him and her mouth was on his.

The kiss took them both by surprise; neither expected what happened next. The impulsive kiss, once sweet and tender, changed to unrestrained passion and then to pure aggressive want. It was as if their bodies took over their reason. Shauna wrapped her arms around Dominik's neck and he encircled her waist, pulling her close.

The kiss was all-consuming passion and beyond. She parted her lips and he delved deep into her mouth. Their tongues twisted and teased, sucked and savored the sudden life-affirming sweetness. The moment was insane, but she couldn't stop herself. This was something she had longed to do for years.

Books by Celeste O. Norfleet

Harlequin Kimani Romance

Sultry Storm
When It Feels So Right
Cross My Heart
Flirting with Destiny
Come Away with Me
Just One Touch
Just One Taste
Mine at Last

CELESTE O. NORFLEET,

a native Philadelphian, has always been artistic, but now her artistic imagination flows through the computer keys instead of a paintbrush. She is a prolific writer for Harlequin Kimani Arabesque and Harlequin Kimani Romance. Her romance novels, realistic with a touch of humor, depict strong, sexy characters and have unpredictable plots and exciting story lines. With an impressive backlist, she continues to win rave reviews and critical praise for her spicy, sexy romances that scintillate as well as entertain. Celeste also lends her talent to the Harlequin Kimani TRU young adult line. Her young adult novels are dramatic fiction, reflecting current issues facing all teens. Celeste has been nominated for and is the winner of numerous awards. She lives in Virginia with her family. You can visit her website, www.celesteonorfleet.wordpress.com, or contact her at conorfleet@aol.com or P.O. Box 7346, Woodbridge, VA 22195-7346.

Mine at Last

CELESTE O. NORFLEET

HARLEQUIN® KIMANI™ ROMANCE

To Fate & Fortune

Recycling programs
for this product may
not exist in your area.

ISBN-13: 978-0-373-86298-6

MINE AT LAST

HARLEQUIN®
www.Harlequin.com

Printed in U.S.A.

Dear Reader,

The Coles family of Key West series has really captured my creative imagination. I hope you're enjoying the wonderfully entertaining characters as much as I am. Writing about their indomitable spirit is a true pleasure. Their close family bond and heartfelt drive to find happiness has inspired me once again. In *Mine at Last* you will meet Dr. Dominik Coles and Shauna Banks. Both are headstrong and focused on a single goal, but getting to it has them battling until the very end. Sit back with a cool drink and enjoy reading how Dominik and Shauna are perfect together. As this series draws to an end, watch for the last story. It's entitled *The Thrill of You.*

And be ready for my next family series, The Buchanans of Alaska. You've met Andre and Chase—now you'll meet the rest of the exciting Buchanan family.

Celeste O. Norfleet

www.celesteonorfleet.wordpress.com

Chapter 1

Shauna Banks drove slowly as she followed the signs that directed her to Key West Medical Center. But she didn't need the signs. She could have found her way in the middle of a category-five hurricane. Chills crawled through her body and the tiny hairs on the back of her neck stood on end. Being here brought back too many bad memories. She had once vowed never to return to this place and she hadn't in almost fifteen years. Now she didn't have a choice. She looked up at the huge structure and took a deep breath.

Coming from another assignment, she was tired and restless, but she had a job to do and there was no alternative. Being her own boss made her solely responsible for the success of her business. Her biggest client, the

Cura Medical Group, needed her professional consulting services. It wasn't until she'd already agreed that she found out which medical center she'd be reviewing. Now, with the faster timetable put in place due to unforeseen circumstances, everything got moved up, including her company's involvement in this process.

Her plan was simple and straightforward—get this over with and leave Key West as soon as possible. To expedite the process, she'd gotten in the night before. Even though she had an appointment to get started the following week, she didn't want to wait. The sooner she got this job over with, the better.

Shauna parked her car as far away from the main entrance as she could. Then she turned the light on and quickly reviewed the notes one last time. She got out and walked toward the emergency doors as if she were condemned and walking to the gallows. Each step sent a spike of pain into her heart. Suddenly, she was seventeen years old again, with her arm draped around her mother's shoulders as they rushed to get help. Lightning flashed, thunder rumbled and rain poured down drenching them, but it didn't matter. All she knew was she'd soon be getting help for her mother. Everything would be okay. She was wrong. That was when it all started, or rather, it all ended for her. But that was a long time ago and she was a different person now.

As soon as she entered the hospital E.R. waiting area, her stomach jumped. She hated this part. The ominous thought of being there made her feel empty and raw. She walked farther in and looked around. At five o'clock in the morning, dim lights and sterile surroundings greeted her. A few people turned to look in her direction but then went back to what they were doing. There was a line at check-in. She waited.

This morning it appeared she had perfect timing. There were a number of people already waiting, plus two families in line in front of her. The first was a couple with two small children. One child, the youngest, was crying miserably in her mother's arms. The other clung sleepily to her father's neck while holding tight to a small stuffed animal.

In front of them was an older Latino couple, already speaking with the nurse at check-in about medical insurance and the man's swollen and bruised arm. Shauna smiled to herself. These two families would give her the perfect opportunity to time them going through the system. She stood behind them listening as nonchalantly as possible.

This was her usual modus operandi—to come early in the morning, before she was expected, to observe how the staff operated and performed. Dressed in jeans, a simple top, sneakers and a baseball cap, she made sure to blend in and go unnoticed. It wasn't exactly being sneaky or underhand; it was more like firsthand reliable scrutiny. They anticipated her arrival next week. It was unofficial, but this was when she saw the real people doing their real jobs, and for good or bad, she evaluated them accordingly.

This was always an E.R.'s first impression. And how they made it was extremely important. Shauna watched and listened as the duty nurse gathered the man's pertinent information. Afterward she quickly assessed the extent of the injury for triage and general patient care. It took only a few minutes. To Shauna's surprise, the process was quick and efficient. She walked away quietly as not to draw attention to herself. Finding a seat away from the check-in desk, she sat and began her more intense study.

This was Key West Medical Center E.R. at five o'clock in the morning. She made a notation in her computer tablet, then proceeded to write a few initial observation notes on general appearance, cleanliness, security, staff attentiveness and overall performance. Having done this dozens of times before, she was detached and methodical and her discipline was unwavering.

Just then a woman walked over and sat down, leaving a seat between them. With much ado the woman heaved a huge leather bag onto the empty seat. Shauna glanced sideways and nodded, giving a polite smile hoping the woman wouldn't talk to her. *Please, don't talk to me. Please, don't talk to me. Please, don't talk to...*

"Hi, I saw you when you came in just now. I've seen you before," the woman said as she rummaged through her big bag and finally pulled out a shiny red apple.

...me. Crap.

Shauna turned at the comment, noticing the older woman leaning to look over her shoulder at the typed screen. She was dressed in flashy party attire and wore way too much makeup and perfume for this time of morning. She was near-skeleton-like thin and her hair was coiffed, teased and lacquered into a huge puff style cemented atop her head. "No, I don't think so. You have me mistaken for someone else."

"I also saw you didn't stop at the check-in desk," the woman said as she rubbed the apple a few times on her dress, then took a huge, juicy bite. "I'm Lindy. We're actually not supposed to eat in here, but I've been sitting here so long that I'm hungry," she whispered and chewed at the same time. She pulled out a second apple and offered it to Shauna.

"Oh, no, thank you," Shauna said, watching her put the apple back into her big bag.

"I see you have one of those new computer tablets that play movies and videos and stuff. I should have brought something more than just this one magazine with me," Lindy said then looked at Shauna's face, puzzled. "So, what's wrong with you? Do you have some kind of chronic illness or something?"

"No, of course not," Shauna said, slightly taken aback.

"Oh, good, 'cause no offence, but I'd have to move if you did. I was in here last month and there was some guy who said he had typhoid fever. Of course, the week before that he said he had malaria." She leaned in closer and whispered, "I think he was crazy or maybe he was one of those hypocrites who think they have all those illnesses."

"You mean a hypochondriac."

"Yeah, that's what I said. I don't see him here right now," Lindy said, then narrowed her eyes and looked closer. "So, what's wrong with you? You don't look all that sick."

"Actually, I'm not here for medical attention," Shauna confessed as her cell phone's email message beeped. She glanced at the message but didn't respond.

"Yeah, I kinda guessed that. I'm also guessing you don't work here, either, right?" Lindy said.

"No," Shauna said, "I don't work here."

"I didn't think so. I know most of the people who work here in E.R. You don't look like a doctor or a nurse. Why are you here?"

Shauna quickly decided to ignore the question. "Really? Then maybe you can tell me about some of the people here. What are they like? You don't have to be exact or anything like that, just general. Do they know their jobs? Are they professional?"

Lindy shrugged. "Yeah, they're all nice. Well, most of them. They're cool, and yeah, they're professional and they know their jobs. They pay attention and do their best to take care of patients when you come in here. But you know there's always craziness going on behind the scenes."

"You mean the lawsuit that's been in the news?" Shauna said.

"Yeah, that and also I hear the hospital is going broke.

I hope not. It would be a shame if they close it down," she said, looking around slowly.

"Sounds like you come here a lot," Shauna said. Lindy nodded. "Did you know Dr. Bowman?" Lindy shrugged hesitantly. Shauna could tell she didn't want to answer her. "You mentioned that you've been waiting a long time. How long have you been sitting here this morning?" Shauna asked.

"About two or three hours," Lindy said nonchalantly.

"What, you've been sitting here for over two hours?" Shauna said in complete astonishment as she quickly made a notation on the computer tablet. "That's ridiculous."

"Nah, it's no big deal."

"Actually, it's a huge deal. That's not supposed to happen. When someone comes into Emergency, they're supposed to get timely medical attention. No one should have to be here that long."

Lindy shrugged. "It's okay. I'm usually here much longer," she said, taking another bite of her apple. "You don't work here and you're not sick, so what are you doing here?"

Shauna decided to hedge and be as vague as possible with her response. "I'm just looking around, checking the place out."

"Oh, I get it. You're one of those."

"One of who?" Shauna asked.

"Hey, look, I know you have a job to do and all—I get that. But seriously, I don't know why y'all keep coming here and hanging around asking questions. What are you looking for? What's wrong with this place?" Lindy asked while looking around. Then she turned for an answer.

Shauna realized her question wasn't rhetorical. Her first instinct was to sidestep the question again, but given the circumstances, she told the truth. "What's wrong with it—I don't know yet. That's why I'm here, to look around and find out," Shauna said. Just then, there was a commotion at the main check-in desk.

A man was taking pictures. Two security guards were called over to confront the man, who seemed adamant about staying. Security was equally determined to make him leave. A few minutes into the dispute another man walked up. The man began taking pictures again and yelling about freedom of the press. The guards eventually escorted the photographer out of the building. Shauna watched the situation play out. "I wonder what that was all about," she said.

Lindy had also shifted her attention to the front area. "Believe it or not, that has happened a lot lately. That same guy was talking to me earlier and asking questions about the E.R. doctors and nurses just like you. Wait, do y'all two know each other?" Lindy asked, looking at Shauna suspiciously.

"No, I've never seen him before," Shauna said defensively.

"Huh," Lindy said, then looked back to the front. "Oh, good, there he is," she said excitedly. "I have to go.

I need to talk to him." She quickly gathered her things back into her bag.

Shauna glanced around, then stopped when she saw a man standing at the check-in desk talking with the nurses and security guards. He was tall, dressed in dark pants and a dark-colored shirt with a hospital badge on his pants belt. He was turned to the side, so that was all she could really see of him. "Does he work here?"

"Oh, honey, does he ever. He is *the* doctor here. You can forget about all those McDreary, McScary, McWhatever knuckleheads playing doctors on those TV shows. He's the real thing. He's gorgeous with money and a heart of gold. Everybody adores him."

"What's his name?"

"I gotta go before he gets away. He's a busy man. It was good talking to you," Lindy said. "See ya."

"Um, maybe we can talk again later," Shauna said quickly, but Lindy had already hurried away. She was headed straight to the check-in desk. She called out just as the doctor was about to walk away. He stopped and turned. Shauna watched, then frowned. Lindy had stepped right in the way and she still couldn't see his face, but there was something about him that seemed very familiar.

A few seconds later, she went back to taking notes specifically centered on tightening security in the E.R. waiting area. Afterward she looked around. Everyone who had been waiting when she arrived was gone and a few new people sat waiting. She noted the time, made a few more notes, then glanced up again.

Lindy was still talking with the group at the check-in desk. Shauna smiled at seeing her. She was in full animation mood with her arms waving and her head bobbing. She laughed loudly and smiled as if she was a teenager again. Then she went quiet and looked at Shauna and nodded her head and smiled. Still watching, Shauna half smiled, then looked down when she heard her cell phone's email message beep again.

She grabbed her phone and checked the message. It was the email she was expecting. She'd gotten the okay she needed to proceed. She replied, outlining the schedule she intended to follow. Just as she pressed the send key, she saw someone standing in front of her. She looked up. Tall, handsome and drop-dead gorgeous was definitely an understatement. He had said something and was waiting for her reply. All she could say was "Huh?"

Chapter 2

Dr. Dominik Coles knew it was going to be one of those days, even before he walked out of the door this morning. He had back-to-back meetings scheduled all morning and afternoon. Bearing that in mind, he stopped at his sister's café before it opened to the public. He took a few minutes to chat and pick up some coffee and pastries for the hospital staff.

The weather certainly didn't help matters much. The hospital was just getting back on its legs after last week's near-miss tropical depression.

Storms threatened and the temperature was headed near ninety degrees again today. There were heavy clouds looming overhead and the threat of a tropical storm in the Gulf turning into a hurricane. This would make people anxious. And with anxiety came mistakes and accidents and inevitably a full E.R.

He stifled a morning yawn as he pulled his car into the reserved lot and parked in his usual space. He shut off the ignition and removed his cell from the car's phone system. He grabbed his case, his coffee and the pastries from the passenger seat and paused a second, feeling the last remnants of cool air-conditioning before opening the car door. As soon as he did, the morning's swell of mugginess hit him. It was barely dawn and the weather was already miserable.

He sighed heavily knowing there was no preparing for the busy day ahead. He locked the car and headed across the empty lot. He looked up at the familiar illuminated sign as he approached the E.R. entrance—Key West Medical Center. This was his home away from home. Pride filled his heart. He'd done good work here and he had saved many lives within these walls and intended to save many more. Just as he passed the sign, it twitched and blinked. He shook his head, making a mental note to call maintenance as soon as he got to his office.

Granted, the hospital wasn't much to look at. The building had problems. It was old and close to falling down around them. Conservatively, it needed a five-million-dollar infusion of cash to get it anywhere near updated. But there was nothing he could do about that. All he could do was help his patients as best he could with optimum care and make sure the numbers balanced at the end of the quarter. Of course, both had become increasingly difficult with everything that had gone on in the past few months.

The previous E.R. director, Harris Bowman, had resigned and then retired amid allegations pertaining to a number of malpractice suits leveled against him. Dominik had taken over as acting director. His new position was a thankless title that afforded him all the perks and gratitude usually reserved for beggars on the street. But feeling sorry for himself wasn't his style. He chose this. He could have refused the post, but doing that would have certainly closed the E.R. and eventually the medical center. He wasn't about to let that happen. The community needed Key West Medical and he intended to keep it open as long as possible.

This morning he needed to take it one step at a time, which meant focusing on the day ahead. His job entailed maintaining a clean working environment and to ensure high-quality patient care. He also reviewed scheduling of his primary-care directors; checked the supply room to make sure the stock was adequately shelved, organized and up-to-date. These were his responsibilities between meetings.

He walked into the E.R. There was a confrontation going on between a man taking pictures and two security guards. It was getting out of hand. "What's going on?" he asked.

Everyone stopped and looked at him. The man with the camera pushed away from the security guard and stepped up to Dominik. "Dr. Coles, I have a few questions for you. Is it true that you knew Dr. Bowman was too old and making sometimes fatal medical mistakes? Were you covering for him, and if so, how long has this been going on?"

"Sir, do you require medical attention?" Dominik asked.

"What? No. I want to know…"

"Then you have no business here. You're gonna have to leave."

"Hey, you can't throw me out. Haven't you ever heard of freedom of the press? I'm within my rights to be here."

"Yes, as a matter of fact, I have heard of the First Amendment. Have you ever heard of trespassing, loitering and illegal entry? Have a nice day," he said, nodding to the guards to continue. The man shouted the whole time. Dominik waited a few seconds as the man continued yelling and then angrily walked across the parking lot.

When the guards returned, he asked if everything was okay. He got a quick report from the nurse at the check-in desk. Satisfied that everything was back to normal, he turned to go to his office. He stopped when he heard his name called.

Dominik turned, recognizing the voice and, of course, the shortened pronunciation of his name. Few called him Dom, usually just his family. But there was also Lindy.

"Dr. Dom, good morning."

He turned, smiling. "Good morning, Lindy. How are you today?"

"Not so good. I've had this pain in my side all night. I came in a few hours ago, but they couldn't find anything, so I thought I had better wait around here and see if it comes back. Also, there's a woman over there writing about you."

"Excuse me?"

"I think she's a reporter," she whispered.

Dominik looked around the waiting room and instantly spotted a woman sitting alone in the back of the large open area. She was focused on writing something on her computer tab. He took a deep breath, then exhaled in exasperation. Her head was down, focused on what she was doing. She wore jeans, T-shirt and a cap pulled low to obscure her face. "Excuse me, Lindy."

He walked over to the woman. She didn't look up. She was still too engrossed in what she was writing on the tablet. She hit one last key, then seemed startled to see him standing there in front of her. She looked up quickly and gasped as her jaw dropped.

He half smiled. He certainly didn't expect to find this stunning beauty beneath the ridiculous disguise. She had no makeup on and still her honey-toasted face shone with brilliant radiance. Her almond-shaped eyes and high cheekbones gave her a decidedly exotic look that always attracted him. Her hair was long and pulled back in a thick ponytail and shoved beneath a cap that had three letters imprinted on the front—*CMG*. But it was her mouth and full lips that drew his immediate attention. Open in the perfect O shape, instantly giving him all kinds of ideas. His body twitched and his pants pulled tight across the front. His physical attraction to her was strong, immediate and unprecedented.

He'd known a few reporters—his sister, Tatiana, was a reporter—and they were a tenacious group whose only focus was the story they were currently chasing. It was a shame because he certainly would like to get to know this one better. But if she was a reporter, he didn't have a choice. She had to go. "Can I help you with something?" he asked, already knowing what she wanted.

Shauna hadn't recovered yet. Her jaw was still dropped and her heart jumped, skipping a few beats. Her stomach lurched and crumbled as if she'd been tossed off the Empire State Building in free fall. She stared up at his half smirking, half stoic expression as the air around her seemed to evaporate. It was him. She knew him from a long time ago—Dominik Coles. He repeated his question. "Huh?" was the best she could muster at that moment as gathering coherent words was apparently impossible.

His eyes narrowed. He wasn't smiling now. "My name is Dr. Coles. Do you need emergency medical attention?" he asked her.

She swallowed hard, finding it difficult to speak. She shook her head, then finally answered, "Um, no."

"Are you waiting for someone who's being seen in the back?"

"No."

"Then may I ask why you're here?"

She considered telling him and then changed her mind. She wasn't ready to end her observations. "I'm just here looking around," she said simply.

"Why?" he asked.

"It's my job."

Dominik took a deep breath and shook his head. Ever since Harris Bowman's lawsuit and the ensuing scandal, the hospital had been crawling with reporters. "Well, you're gonna have to do your job someplace else. This isn't a library, a social club or a coffeehouse media center. You can't just walk in, have a seat and chill out. So, come on, get your things. It's time to go."

"Wait, are you kidding me?" she said. "You're throwing me out of the E.R.? You can't do that."

"Do I look like I'm kidding? You don't need emergency service, so you can't just come in here off the street and have a seat. This waiting room is for our patients and their families. Government regulations do not stipulate reporters are allowed to harass patients in my E.R."

"Reporter, no, you don't understand…"

"As a matter of fact, I do understand," he interrupted. "You're here staked out to try to get a story, just like your photographer friend we just escorted out. Put your tablet away, get your things and leave here before I ask security to escort you out, too." He glanced down at her computer tablet, the hospital's name typed prominently across the screen. "And whatever it is you want to know, I have no comment and neither does anyone else."

She hastily covered her tablet and grabbed her brief-case. As she picked it up, her wallet and keys fell out. She grabbed her wallet. He picked up her keys and handed them to her. She took them and, along with her tablet, secured them in the briefcase. The last thing she needed was for him to see what she was writing or ask for iden-tification. "I'm not here to…"

"Come on, your photographer friend's waiting for you."——

"But I'm not with him and I'm not a reporter," she said.

He turned and motioned for the two security guards standing by to come over. "Yeah, that's what the last guy just said. He was trying to get into the back to take pictures," Dominik stated to Shauna,

"You're making a mistake," she protested.

"Lady, I don't make mistakes," he said just as secu-rity arrived at his side. "Gentlemen, please escort this reporter off the premises."

"I'm telling you, I'm not a reporter," Shauna repeated as she put her briefcase on her shoulder and stood. The security guards moved behind her. "Fine, I'm leaving."

"Thank you. Have a nice day."

Dominik watched as the security guards followed her through the automatic doors. His gaze followed her across the parking lot to her car.

At his desk, he turned on his computer and opened his schedule. His first meeting, with a new pharmaceutical representative, was in thirty-five minutes. That gave him just enough time to quickly review and assess the last few patients who were admitted to the E.R. Just as he opened the computer file, there was a knock on his door.

"Yeah, come in," he said without looking up. The door opened and his assistant, Nora Rembrandt, smiled and then shook her head in sympathy.

"Good morning," Nora said, "I hope you're ready for a crazy one, 'cause it's gonna be one of those days already. You're wanted out in the pit—in exam room snake-eyes two, sexy-legs six and lucky number thirteen. And heads-up, security is on full alert. Someone jimmied the lock on the hospital records room sometime early this morning and also someone tried to break into a third-floor drug cabinet again."

Dominik nodded and stood to leave. He was surprised he was getting better at Nora's bingo-calling jargon. He understood her perfectly. "Yeah, you're right. It's going to be one of those days."

His desk phone rang. Nora answered, agreed, then hung up. "It's already starting. It's Dr. Gilman and she wants you in her office at you earliest convenience."

He nodded, stood and walked out, going to the E.R. to visit the patients she'd told him about. Afterward he headed up to the administrative office. He pushed open the glass door and strolled into the reception area. No was there, so he headed to the main offices. Dr. Gilman's door was open. He knocked and walked in. The sweltering heat hit him immediately. The office was stifling. Gilman was at her desk with her glasses on and a large portable fan turned off behind her. Her desk was piled high with files and paperwork.

"Good morning, Margaret," Dominik said, frowning. "That's a lot of paperwork."

"Good morning, Dominik," she said, then glanced up at the two huge stacks piled high on the side of her desk. She nodded and sighed heavily. "Yeah, these are some of the files requested by the Cura Group. The first and second auditors finished up and now they're sending their consultant in next week to do the final. I don't know who this person is, but they pull a lot of weight in getting this through. Come in and have a seat."

He walked over and sat down as she began rearranging the papers and folders further to the side of her desk. "Does not look like a fun job," he said.

"Believe me, it's not, but after reviewing what the last two teams did, they specifically wanted to examine and look these over. The majority are Bowman's E.R. records. Something obviously stood out, but it completely eludes me."

"So, what happened to the air-conditioning in here?" he asked.

"Maintenance has been working on it for the last two days. We need a new system, but that costs money and right now funds are scarce. Okay, busy day ahead. It looks like someone tried to break into the medical records office this morning."

"Yes, I heard. Has security checked the video yet?"

"Yes, they're reviewing the video now." She took off

her glasses and tossed them on the desk. "I gotta tell you, Dominik, this is the last thing I need this morning. The Cura Group's reviewer will be here next week and I can't have this happening when they're here. Do you have any idea what this would do to our chances of having this buyout go through?"

She stood and walked to the window anxiously, then came back to her desk and leaned on her chair. "This thing is out of control, not to mention it's a public-relations nightmare. Who's going to come here if their medical records are free to the public? The publicity is killing us. And now we have reporters sneaking in here every five minutes speaking with an unofficial source close to the situation. What the hell is that?" The rant continued for another few minutes before she stopped and looked at him. "I heard you had an unwanted visitor in the E.R. this morning."

"Which time?"

"The reporter," she said curiously. "Why, were there more?"

"Yes, we had a couple of reporters lurking around. One tried taking pictures of the E.R. and the other was interviewing people in the waiting area."

"I hope you didn't throw them out physically."

"Not exactly, but the thought had crossed my mind." She looked at him sternly. "No, of course we didn't throw them out. They were asked to leave nicely. One decided to cause some trouble—make a scene. We handled it."

"And the other?"

"She left quietly."

"Good. Damn, I wish they'd leave us alone."

Dominik shook his head. "I don't think that's gonna happen anytime soon. The story is too juicy. The hospital's chief E.R. director named in three medical malpractice suits is too scandalous to pass up."

"Apparently," she said, sitting back down. "My phone's been ringing off the hook with reporters asking for interviews and comments. And the damn lawyers can't do anything about it—freedom of speech, who needs it? But enough of that. I called you in this morning because we need your help."

"Sure. What can I do?"

"As I mentioned, the Cura Medical Group will be sending their consultant in to review us for the next few weeks. They're going to be observing the E.R. specifically."

Dominik shook his head. This was the last thing he needed—an interfering bureaucrat nosing around asking questions all day. It was a waste of time. "Margaret…"

"I'm also going to need you to be very hands-on with them."

This was so not what he wanted—to babysit some corporate hatchet. "Margaret…"

"Dominik, I know your feelings about this buyout. I understand your concerns and I even agree with some of them. I also know that I don't have to tell you how important this is to the medical center. We need this to go well. As you know, according to an inside source at Cura, we haven't fared too well so far. And this malpractice thing with Bowman is only making matters worse."

"That's ridiculous. This medical center is one of the best in the state. What we lack in funding we more than make up for in heart and dedication."

"Heart and dedication don't pay the bills, my friend. Anyway, be that as it may, we need to make a good impression and I need you on your top game. They're going to be in your department. So, charm them, wow them, woo them. I don't care what you do. Just make it happen."

"If I didn't know any better, I'd say you were pimping me out."

"If that works, fine. You have my blessing."

"I'll tell you what—I'll do my job as always. But you know my feelings about the Cura Group." His cell phone beeped. He checked the message and stood up. "I gotta go. Are we done?"

"Yes," she said, "and, Dominik, remember, we need this. Thanks."

"You're welcome. Have a good one." He walked out.

Chapter 3

Shauna walked into the hospital E.R. for the second time that day. Now she was there officially. Just as she'd done ten hours earlier, she stood in line and listened for a few minutes, then stepped aside and looked for a seat. But unlike before, this time she sat closer to the check-in desk, knowing she'd see and hear everything going on. After sitting, she looked around cautiously. Lindy wasn't there and hopefully no one else would bother her as she watched, listened and did her job.

It wasn't exactly voyeurism. It was just paying very close attention. She saw everything. It was her job to be observant. The waiting room's wide-open space afforded her the perfect view as pain and suffering continued all around her. A small child wept in his mother's arms. She rocked slowly, hoping to ease what anguish she could. An old man coughed and held a dirty, crumpled handkerchief to his mouth. Two other people sat anxiously waiting to be called, one nauseous and the other holding a bleeding nose.

As usual, Shauna steeled herself from the emotional trial of empathy. Instead, she remained completely objective and distant to those around her. She barely blinked an eye hearing a child crying or seeing a bleeding wound. She pulled out her computer tablet and began working. Names were called and people got up and disappeared behind a secured door accessed only by the nurse at check-in desk or a swipe of a key card. For the next hour and a half, she watched and wrote what she saw and didn't see. She noted suggestions and remarked on various situations.

Her job was the last step before finalizing the buyout, and so far, she wasn't impressed. Midway through a reference to expedite the triage process, her cell phone vibrated. She pulled it out and glanced at the caller ID. "Hey, Pearl," she said quietly as she looked around. "How are you? Everything okay?"

"No, everything's not okay. I'm losing my mind and I'm bored out of my skull. This retirement thing is for the birds. I'm up early because I've gotten up early every day of my life since I was fourteen years old. And what do I do? Twiddle my thumbs all day. Where's the sense in that? When are you getting here?"

Shauna smiled and chuckled to herself. Pearl Tyson

was a heavyset woman with long, thick black hair that she proudly told everyone took years to grow and she was never cutting. She grew up in foster care and became extremely successful on her own terms. She was Shauna's mother's best friend years ago. They lived next to each other before all the craziness started, and out of all her mother's friend's, she was the only one to stand by her side when the trouble came. "I'm here now. I got in late last night. I was going to call you this weekend."

"You should have called me last night. I'm going crazy here."

"Why don't you watch some television?"

"Yeah, right," she said sarcastically. "Five hundred TV channels and there's not a single thing worth watching on any of them. I swear if I see one more reality show or one more morning or afternoon chitchat talk show yapping about mindless celebrity and want-to-be-celebrity nothing, I'm going to throw the TV out of the window."

Shauna chuckled and shook her head. When said by most people, the comment would be just an open, empty threat. But coming from Pearl Tyson, it was quite possibly true. Pearl was the only person she knew in Key West now. All of her old so-called friends from high school had long since shown their colors. But Pearl had stayed by her family's side for years. Because both her parents were gone, Pearl, a childless orphan herself, had stepped into the role as Shauna's pseudomother and had been at her side ever since.

She was there through college and when Shauna opened her own successful medical consulting business. She was Shauna's biggest fan. She even helped her land one of her company's biggest clients, Cura Medical Group. The Cura Group bought medical facilities. Their newest potential acquisition was the Key West Medical Center. This brought her full circle back to Key West. "No, don't toss the TV."

"All right, enough of this. So, what are you up to today?"

"Right now I'm sitting in the E.R. checking the place out."

"Don't you usually do that earlier in the mornings?" Pearl said.

"Yes, I do and I did, but…" she hedged.

"But what?" Pearl prompted.

"I was interrupted and then it got a little complicated."

"Complicated, what do you mean, 'complicated'?" Pearl asked.

Shauna took a deep breath and exhaled slowly. This wasn't exactly what she wanted to talk about, but she knew Pearl would understand. "It's no big deal. I got thrown out, that's all," she said, saving her document and exiting her file.

Pearl chuckled. "What, you got thrown out? What did you do?"

"Nothing. It was a mistake. They thought I was a reporter."

"Why did they think that?"

"It's a long story and not important."

"Fine, don't tell me. So, who threw you out? Security?"

"Yeah, with the insistence of one of the doctors here," she said.

Pearl chuckled again. "Oh, my God, this is so much better than daytime TV. So, which doctor?"

"Does it matter?"

"Hell, yeah, it matters. Come on. I'm bored, I need details."

Shauna sighed again. "Dr. Dominik Coles."

"I know Dr. Coles. He works at the doctors' clinic—tall and gorgeous, right?"

"Yeah, something like that," Shauna said.

"Exactly like that. So, what made him think you were a reporter?"

"If I had to guess, I'd say that some busybody told him I was asking her questions about the staff. They're pretty paranoid around here."

"Oh, yeah, right, because of the malpractice lawsuits."

"Yeah, that would be my guess."

"Well, anyway, you're back. When are you going to officially start the auditing process?"

"I'm going to meet with the hospital administrator, Dr. Gilman, today, as soon as I leave here."

"I thought the appointment was for next week."

"It is, but because I got the go-ahead email report early this morning, I figured I might as well get started.

Cura Medical is anxious to get this one finalized one way or another."

"Yeah, I read in the newspaper that they're really interested in buying Key West Medical Center. The paper said that an inside source was quoted saying that the accounting department's report went through and the numbers checked out. To tell you the truth, after everything with the E.R., I expected worse."

"You can't always trust the accounting numbers," Shauna said skeptically. "Besides, that's just surface numbers reporting. The books never give an accurate depiction of feasibility. And I know how easily the books can be manipulated. I've seen it done a hundred times."

"True," Pearl said.

"Cura Medical could be buying a ship sinking into a bottomless pit."

"Or they could be buying a gold mine," Pearl countered.

"True, but in the meantime, turn off the TV and read a book."

"I've read everything in the house."

"What about downloaded books on the ereader?" Shauna asked.

"Yeah, I guess I could do that," Pearl said.

"Download a book and I'll be there this evening. I'll take you to dinner."

"No, I'll cook dinner here. Seven o'clock okay?"

"Yes, it sounds perfect. I'll pick up dessert. Is there anything in particular you'd like?"

"Go to Nikita's Café on Main Street. Everything there is delicious."

"Okay, sounds good. I'll see you at…"

"Help me! Help me! Please, somebody help me!"

Shauna, hearing the pleas for help, stopped speaking and looked up, as did everyone in the immediate area. A man had rushed in with a woman barely in his arms. He struggled carrying her and then crumbled to his feet as he approached the desk. Shauna stood and watched.

"Pearl, I'll see you at seven. Bye."

"Please, somebody help her. It's my wife—she needs help now."

Instantly, the nurse at the check-in desk rushed from behind the counter. As she approached, the man fell to the floor with the woman on top of him. Seconds later the doors from the triage area burst open and security appeared, followed by two nurses. A doctor in a white coat quickly followed on their heels.

Shauna grabbed her things and stepped up to watch, along with a few other people. The doctor and nurses began helping the woman while asking the man questions about what happened. A few seconds later, Shauna looked up and saw Dominik come out and push through those standing around. "Get these people back," he ordered to security, "and get a gurney out here now. What's the status?" He knelt down beside the other doctor as he quickly examined the woman, assessing her symptoms.

Security began moving people back to the main waiting area. Shauna managed to avoid them while staying close to the situation.

"Eyes and mouth are swollen, breathing's shallow and labored, heart palpitations, pulse erratic," the doctor said on a rush, "onset severe anaphylactic shock."

"Sir, what happened?" Dominik asked the man who seemed to now be in shock, too. He just stared at his wife, motionless. "Sir, we need your help here. What happened to her?" he repeated.

"I don't know. I don't know, we were eating dinner and she just started scratching her face and wheezing. Then she said she couldn't breathe and was grabbing at her throat and gasping for air, but she's not asthmatic. She stood up and then fell into my arms. I grabbed her and drove here as fast as I could."

"What's her name?" Dominik asked.

"Um, um, Anna. Anna Gomez. No, it's Anna Carpenter. We just got married. We're on our honeymoon. Please, help her."

"Anna. Anna, can you hear me?" the other doctor asked. The woman moaned and rolled her head erratically.

"She's nonresponsive," Dominik said. "Let's get her to the back."

"Anna, hold on. We're gonna get you better. Sir, what medications is she taking?" the doctor asked the man.

"I don't know. I can't remember. I..."

"Where's that gurney?" Dominik yelled over his shoulder. Just then, a hospital gurney burst through the doors followed by another nurse. Dominik and the doctor picked up the woman and placed her on the narrow bed. "Come on, let's go," he ordered as the nurses began pushing the gurney back through the doors. The other doctor ran alongside. Dominik stayed.

While everyone else watched the gurney pass through the back doors, Shauna watched Dominik as he guided the anxious husband to the side. They spoke quietly for a few minutes, then Dominik nodded and asked a nurse to escort him to the inside waiting area. When the tense situation passed, he looked around at all the concerned faces. He spoke to security, then turned to go to the back.

That was when he spotted Shauna. He paused a brief instant and stared at her. They connected and there was the barest hint of recognition, but the glimmer vanished almost as quickly as it appeared. She opened her mouth to speak, but then his cell beeped. He grabbed it off his belt, slid his key card and quickly disappeared through the back doors. Just that fast, he was gone.

Shauna looked around. Although there was a definite buzz centered on what had just happened, it was also evident that everything was back to as it was. A nurse stepped out and called out two names, and instantly, the tenseness of the past five minutes was gone and everyone went back to waiting for medical attention.

Shauna left the E.R. and headed out to the main hospital lobby. She took the elevator to the administrative offices. She pulled out her Cura Medical Group lanyard and placed it around her neck. Shauna took a deep breath and stilled her nerves.

She wasn't sure it was a good idea to come here. Perhaps she should have passed on this assignment and let someone else take it. But she didn't. She was a professional and it was too late now. Cura was already several months into the process. She couldn't back out now without questions being asked and damaging her reputation in the process. No, she had to see this through. And more important, it was time to put all this behind her.

The rest of the hospital's operations and assessments had been completed and this was the last thing that had to be done—the overall performance and the E.R. evaluation. If she filed a bad report, the Cura Medical Group would pass on the deal.

The elevator doors opened and she walked down the narrow corridor with the high-polished floors. The walls were lined with poster-size pictures of children in medical outfits helping other children. At the end of the hall was a glass door. She pushed through and came to an open area with a woman sitting at a reception desk.

She looked up and half smiled. "This office is hospital administration. How may I help you?"

"Good afternoon, I'd like to speak with Dr. Gilman, please."

The woman looked Shauna up and down with her nose perched a few inches in the air. Her assessment was slow and methodical. Shauna assumed she was trying to figure out if she was a reporter. She could have saved the woman trouble, but this was also part of her examination—office staff serviceability. "Your name and company?" the woman finally asked tightly.

"My name is Shauna Banks. I'm from the Cura Medical Group. Dr. Gilman should be expecting me."

The receptionist, wearing thick, red-framed glasses and matching lipstick, opened her computer screen and typed something in. She looked up at Shauna and smiled triumphantly. "Your appointment is for next week. You're early," she said snidely.

"Yes, I am."

"It's Friday afternoon and Dr. Gilman is very busy."

"I understand. Please inform Dr. Gilman that I'm here."

The woman sighed and picked up the phone. She pressed a few keys, then waited a second or two. "I'm sorry, there's no answer in the office. Perhaps you can come back at your scheduled appointment time next week. I'm sure Dr. Gilman will be available at that time."

Shauna smiled. "Fine, thank you. Have a good weekend," she said, then turned to leave. As she pushed through the glass doors, she passed an older woman quickly coming into the office. They smiled politely at each other as Shauna continued to the elevator. She got in and removed her lanyard. Moments later the doors opened. Security was standing there waiting for her.

"Ma'am, we'd like to escort you back to Dr. Gilman's office."

Shauna nodded. "Sure, thanks." She stepped back into

the elevator with two huge security guards at her sides. The elevator ascended in silence. As soon as the doors opened, the same older woman she passed moments earlier smiled and extended her hand. "Good afternoon. Welcome to Key West Medical Center."

"Thank you," Shauna said as she stepped out, leaving the guards to take the elevator back down. "Dr. Gilman?"

"Yes, I am Margaret Gilman," the woman said happily.

"Dr. Gilman, I'm Shauna Banks, representing the Cura Medical Group. You're expecting me."

"Yes, yes, indeed I am. Ms. Banks, please come into the office." They pushed through the glass doors. Shauna spared a quick glance at the receptionist, who was surprisingly engulfed in typing something in the computer. "Ms. Banks, I'm so sorry about the mix-up earlier at the reception desk. I'm afraid we're a bit cautious because of the reporters. We've had every scam and trick in the book thrown at us for interviews and bogus copycat lawsuits. Had I known you were coming in early, I would have had someone escort you directly to my office."

"I'm afraid that's all part of my job. I'm here to observe and report my experiences with your staff and service, as well," Shauna said.

"Yes, of course. I understand," she said, opening her office door. A blast of heat hit them instantly. "I'm sorry about the heat. The air-conditioning in this office is on the fritz. Feel free to take off your jacket. Please, have a seat. Can I get you something cold to drink?"

"No, thank you, I'm fine. This is just a preliminary meeting to give you an idea of what I'll be doing the next few weeks. Just as with my previous associates, I would appreciate it if my association with Cura is confidential except to you and your E.R. department head."

"Yes, of course."

"It's very difficult to get a fair and unbiased appraisal of your hospital staff and procedures if everyone is on their best behavior."

Dr. Gilman nodded repeatedly. "I understand completely."

"Good. Now, I understand due to recent very unfortunate circumstances surrounding your E.R., you are without a department head. I can tell you that Cura is very concerned about this situation. By all accounts the buyout process was looking favorable, but this new development has definitely put a wrinkle in the process. Without an acceptable director, I can't completely do my job, and it would be very unlikely that I can…"

"Well, actually, Ms. Banks, we've recently elected an acting department head. He's accepted the position and we're thrilled and honored to have him. He's a brilliant doctor with very deep roots in Key West and in this community. His medical record is exceptional and his ethics are without blemish. He's extremely respected throughout the medical community."

"I see. Okay, that's wonderful and a very positive

step in the right direction. Hopefully we can complete this process within the next few weeks. So, that said, might it be possible to meet your new acting E.R. director today?"

"Yes, of course, definitely. I can have him here in a few minutes," Dr. Gilman said, then picked up her phone to call. Just then, there was a knock on the door. "Come in," she called out. A young woman opened the door and walked in.

"Excuse me, Dr. Gilman. The attorneys are here for your five-thirty teleconference with the board of trustees. It's set up in the main conference room."

"Oh, no, it completely slipped my mind," she said, frowning. "Ms. Banks, I really need to speak with our attorneys. If you'll excuse me, I should be no more than fifteen to twenty minutes."

"Yes, of course. Our meeting wasn't scheduled. I completely understand. Take as much time as you need."

"Thank you for being so understanding."

Shauna began gathering her things. "I can leave and come back."

"Oh, no, that won't be necessary. Please, wait right here. I'll have the acting head of the E.R. department, Dr. Coles, join you," she said, nodding to her assistant to make it happened. "The two of you can meet and plan out the next few weeks together and…"

Shauna's stomach had dropped and her eyes had widened. "Wait, excuse me, who did you say was the E.R. head?" Shauna asked hesitantly.

"Dr. Coles, Dominik Coles. He's our new acting E.R. department head. He'll be right here."

The sound of his name stopped her heart. She froze in place.

Chapter 4

The offhand "It's gonna be one of those days" remark Dominik made earlier that morning turned out to be a gross understatement. He'd been running around since dawn and every minute of his day had been rationed out to paperwork, lawyers, staff and intermediate medical services. He was a bureaucratic paper pusher. Years in medical school and intense training had been wasted to sitting behind a desk and on the phone placating staff and begging for more money from the powers that be who had nothing to spare.

He sat back and looked at his desk, taking a much-needed moment to chill. There was a never-ending battle going on pitting him against a massive montage of need-to, have-to and should-have-been-done-six-weeks-ago facing him. Making headway was more like running backward up a steep mountain on roller skates in the middle of a snowstorm.

He tossed his pen down on the desk and rolled his neck from side to side. Since taking over this position, he'd been faced with every imaginable no-win situation. There were irregular stockroom shortages, underpaid, undertrained staff, daily threats of walkouts and work slowdowns, and of course the lawsuit of the wrongful death filed just before he took over the position. It was a respectable job, but he was a doctor through and through. And right now, playing doctor, as he so often put it, had been put on hold for a while.

His phone rang.

"Can it wait until Monday morning? I'm meeting my chief nursing officer in fifteen minutes," he said, glancing at his watch.

"All right, I'm on my way," Dominik said, then hung up. The first thing he thought was there was another legal charge against the E.R. department. Nowadays they averaged two a week since the news reported the scandal a few months ago. He grabbed his cell phone and dialed his brother's number as he headed out of the office. Mikhail picked up on the first ring.

"Yo, what's up? Don't tell me you're canceling on tonight."

"No, not canceling, but it looks like I'm gonna be running late. I have to meet with Gilman and I have no idea what's up, so I don't know how long it's gonna take."

"All right, I'll stop by there on my way. If you're ready, fine. If not, I'll head out without you."

"Sounds good. See you later," Dominik said, disconnecting. He spotted Donna Pullman sitting at a computer console. He sat beside her. She looked at him and shook her head.

"I don't want to hear it," she said.

"Gilman wants me in her office now."

"You know, this is wrong," she said.

"I know, but trust me, we're gonna get this done. Just let me take care of this and I'll be back and we'll talk."

Donna shook her head. "This is the same as before. What is it in the E.R. department-head job description to ignore us? Bowman did the same thing. I expected better from you."

"Donna, this is me. You've always taken me at my word and I've never given you reason to stop. I will always respect you and your staff. You know this. I *will* be back and we *will* talk."

She nodded. "Fine. Monday morning," she said.

He nodded and left. As he headed to the main steps to the executive level, he heard someone say his name.

"Dr. Coles, I just wanted to thank you for everything. They have Anna up on the second floor. The doctor said she'll be okay and they have her in overnight for observation."

"Good. How's she doing?" Dominik asked.

"Better, much better. She woke up earlier and sounded like herself again. My wife and I appreciate what you did for us. I don't know what we would have done if this E.R. wasn't here."

Dominik nodded. "You're very welcome. Why don't you get some rest? Talk to the nurse if you'd like to stay here with your wife tonight."

"Thanks a lot, Doctor," he said, shaking hands.

"You take care," Dominik said, heading toward the steps. Just as he opened the door, his assistant saw him.

"Hey, what are you still doing down here? Dr. Gilman's assistant is looking for you."

Dominik looked at his watch. "Yeah, I'm on my way now. What's going on?"

Nora shrugged. "I hear she's meeting with the hospital attorney about the lawsuits. What else?"

"An attorney. All right, thanks," Dominik said, then shook his head ruefully thinking about the Cura Medical Group as he hurried up the stairs. As far as he was concerned, the Cura Group was a pack of vultures circling the hospital with greed in their eyes. The buyout had begun months ago. They promised new jobs and a revitalization of the hospital and the community. What Dominik saw was another private investment corporation intent on making money for shareholders on the backs of the needy and infirm. He knew companies like them. They were interested in one thing— making money.

He walked into the executive office and saw the receptionist at her desk. She was talking on the phone.

Dominik pointed toward Gilman's office. She nodded and motioned for him to go in.

As soon as he opened the door, he saw a woman standing at the window leaning back against the ledge. Her head was turned to the window. She seemed engrossed in her thoughts. He just watched.

For the first time in a long time, he felt a pull to just admire the perfectly shaped form in front of him. As a doctor he'd long since learned to distance himself from physical appearance. One body looked much like the next. He didn't see color or shape or size; he saw pain and suffering and felt the need to heal. But watching her pressed his thoughts in a completely different direction. Her body spoke to him and he heard every single word it said.

Dressed in a sleeveless, formfitting, knee-length, dark blue dress with stylish matching high heels and a thick belt, she looked stunning. Her hair was pulled up off her long, slim neck and twisted with a clip. She wore a large necklace and small earrings with no rings or other jewelry. But it was what he didn't see that interested him. Her neckline was high and the dress was low. The only bare skin he saw was her arms and long, shapely legs. Most women dressed way too obviously for him. She was understated and he definitely liked what he saw.

He nodded absently as if to answer a question stagnated in his mind. Yes, it had been a long time for him, too long. By no respects was he a monk, nor did he live a celibate life. Women came and went in his life, but his time and dedication were always focused on the hospital and his passion to heal. Most didn't understand that passion.

As an E.R. doctor he worked for fourteen hours straight. But as the acting emergency-department director, his workday usually extended to eighteen or twenty hours a day. Basically, he worked and went home to sleep. There was no time for anything else. His job was demanding and took everything he had. He had no social life, he seldom saw his family and friends, and dating was completely out of the picture. He knew he had to unwind soon or he'd probably explode.

Shauna turned and looked up, surprised to see Dominik standing in the center of the room. She didn't realize he'd come in. She opened her mouth to speak but nothing came out. He smiled and all of a sudden she felt as if she was back in high school again. Apparently crushes never quite went away.

"Good afternoon," he said, smiling seductively.

Her stomach trembled. The low, sexy rumble of his deep voice was still intoxicating. She hadn't expected her reaction to hearing his voice to be so unsettling. "Hello," she said.

"My name is Dr. Coles, Dominik, and you are?" he asked, crossing the room toward her. He walked with a cool, confident stride that nearly took her breath away. He extended his hand to shake as he approached.

"Shauna, Shauna Banks," she said, leaning away from the windowsill and taking a few steps toward him. She reached out to take his offered hand. They shook politely, but then they each held on an instant longer than necessary. Shauna's insides began to simmer. Just having him look at her made all those old feelings come back. It was so long ago, but right now it felt as if it was yesterday. Realizing it, she quickly released his hand and then stepped back. "I was here earlier..."

"Yes, I know. I saw you. You were in the E.R."

"Yes, I was there when the man brought his wife in. Anaphylactic shock, I believe. How is she?"

He smiled. "Sorry, I can't discuss patient care."

"Yes, of course," she said and halted. "I didn't mean to imply... I just meant that I hope she's better. I'm sure you took good care of her and I didn't mean that I wanted her health history or anything like that." She eased away, realizing she was babbling. "Um, as I was saying, I was in the E.R. earlier this afternoon and..."

"You were here early this morning, as well," he interrupted knowingly as he moved closer.

She opened her mouth to speak, then closed it.

"Although," he continued, "you were dressed far less professionally. I think I like this look better." He slowly gazed down the full length of her body.

She was surprised. She didn't expect he'd recognize her from the early-morning disguise. And his open appraisal and obvious flirting were driving her crazy. "Yes, that's right. You threw me out thinking I was a reporter."

"Obviously you're not or you wouldn't be here now."

"No, I'm not."

"So, what was this morning all about?" he asked. She didn't answer. He nodded. "No need to answer. I'll assume you got lost on your way up here and now you're waiting for Dr. Gilman," he said, moving to stand beside her, facing the window. He looked out at the open skyline. It had rained earlier, but now it seemed that the sun would be making its first appearance in several days.

"No," she said. "Actually, I've been waiting for you."

He turned and leaned back against the windowsill as she looked straight ahead at the bookshelf against the far wall. His smile broadened as he gazed at her profile. "You say that like you really mean it," he said.

She turned to look at him. Then, realizing how her comment sounded, she blushed and turned away again. "That's not how it was intended."

"Are you sure?" he said.

She turned to him again. All the air in the room seemed to have been vacuumed out. She took a slow, deep breath. "Yes, I'm sure," she said, tightening her stance.

"Do you ever loosen up?"

"What?"

"You seem so tight. Do you ever relax and loosen up?"

"No, I don't loosen up."

He nodded as a few seconds passed and neither spoke. "So, Ms. Banks, because you've been waiting for me, what can I do for you this afternoon?"

"I'm a consultant working with the Cura Medical Group and I'd like you to show me around the E.R."

His expression instantly changed as he stepped back and shook his head. His eyes hardened. She knew the reaction well. Most doctors had the same problem with her, or rather, with her occupation. She audited hospitals, medical centers and doctors. As far as they were concerned, she was the enemy, the one who popped their demigod bubble.

"You were there earlier. You know the way," he said. The icy cut of his gaze and the coldness in his voice chilled her even in the overheated office.

She nodded. "Are you going to make this difficult?"

"I'm not sure yet," he said as his eyes narrowed.

"Okay, I'll bite. What's the problem? You were in full charm-and-seduction mode up until I mentioned the company I represent."

He smiled, then chuckled. "I assure you, Ms. Banks, that was not my seduction mode. Had it been, you would have certainly known. Would you like to see seduction mode?"

Again, she was speechless. She took a deep breath. She knew answering him—any answer—would send this conversation to a totally different level. She knew she wasn't ready for that. "As I said, I'm a consultant working for the Cura Medical Group. I'm here to…"

"You're here to evaluate me," he said, taking a step back.

"No, I'm here to evaluate the Key West Medical Center, specifically the emergency department."

"Same difference," he tossed over his shoulder as he walked away from her.

"No, it's not the same at all," she assured him as she followed him around to the front of the desk. "I'm guessing that you obviously don't want the Cura Medical Group here, do you?"

"No."

"May I ask why?"

"I don't want this medical center to be ripped apart, and knowing your Cura, there's a good chance that will happen. Hospitals and clinics have a tendency to close down right after the Cura Group steps in to save them."

Shauna shook her head. "You have your facts wrong. The Cura Group did not close the hospitals."

"No, but they resold them. The result was the same."

"I'm sure those were very unique cases..."

"...that happened three times, the last three times."

It was obvious he'd done his homework. Cura had resold the last three medical facilities even though she specifically warned against it, knowing that they'd thrive with the right kind of leadership. "I've read the initial reports. Whether you know it or not, a lucrative buy is the best chance this medical center has to continue. It's vulnerable, and if Cura doesn't purchase it, it may go under."

"The devil you know or the devil you don't."

"Hardly," she said.

"We've been doing just fine without Cura or any other private corporation where the faceless shareholders have a stake in patients' health care. We'll continue to do fine. Tell me what happens when the dividends drop too low—do you kick patients out of their beds and rent out the rooms as a weekend spa?"

She laughed and shook her head. His stubbornness knew no bounds. "Why can't you just see that you need this? At this point you don't have a choice."

"I see enough," he said more tensely than before.

"I don't think so. The Cura Group operates over fifty quality health-care facilities up and down the East Coast. I have personally recommended they purchase twenty medical centers, hospitals, clinics and doctors' offices. And I'm proud to say they are top-notch. Their medical staffs are dedicated professionals and Cura's support staff is unparalleled. Cura's goal is to improve, with exceptional health service, the health of every community they enter. Their national, regional and local ranking is unmatched."

"That's quite a speech."

"If you weren't so obstinate, you'd see all the benefits of selling and coming here."

"How many people will lose their jobs?"

"Excuse me?"

"In your new regime, how many families will suffer?"

She shook her head. "You act like they're coming here to bully and take over—like they're the enemy."

"If Cura is anything like you…"

"Meaning?" she said tightly.

"It takes more than a balanced bottom line to make a hospital work. It takes compassion, caring and empathy. It takes not walking in here with a chip on your shoulder the size of a two-by-four. It means being fair and reasonable without forgetting the human factor. There's nothing at all wrong with this E.R. or this medical center, and I'll do everything in my power to save it from Cura."

"Fine, and I'll do everything in my power to save it from ineptness, even if that means closing it down."

"Do you know what your problem is?"

"Tell me, Doctor, what's my problem?"

"Your problem is…" he began.

Shauna reached back to lean her hand on the desk and knocked over the huge pile of folders and papers. Everything tumbled and fell to the floor. "Crap," she muttered, looking completely mortified at the mess she'd made. She quickly bent down to pick them up. Grateful for the distraction, she needed to get her emotions under control.

"Here, I got it," Dominik said as he walked back to help her.

When the last paper was picked up, he stood and held out his hand to her. She took it and stood up, too close for comfort. Chest to chest she looked up into his dark, soulful eyes. Her heart stumbled and every nerve ending in her body tingled. Suddenly the high school crush she remembered from so long ago was standing right here in front of her. All she had to do was reach out and touch him. She licked her lips. An instant later she grabbed him and her mouth was on his.

The kiss took them both by surprise. Then neither expected what happened next. The impulsive kiss, once sweet and tender, changed to unrestrained passion and then to pure aggressive want. It was as if their bodies took over their reason. Shauna wrapped her arms around Dominik's neck and he encircled her waist, pulling her close.

The kiss was all-consuming passion and beyond. She parted her lips and he delved deep into her mouth. Their tongues twisted and teased, sucked and savored the sudden life-affirming sweetness. The moment was insane but she couldn't stop herself. This was something she had longed to do for years.

He took a step and pressed her back against the front of the desk. A few papers fell to the carpet again, but she didn't care. This was feeling too good to be true and her mind was wrapped too tightly in the pleasurable sensation of his mouth on hers. He kissed as if he'd invented it and her body responded to his every move.

His hand came up to her breast and squeezed gently. She moaned. He groaned. The kiss deepened. Her hand reached down to feel the imminent hardness between his legs. His excitement was growing more evident by the second. She shuddered inside. It was intense. It was fierce. It was everything she'd ever wanted and imagined. But she knew this was wrong. It was unprofessional, but it felt so damn good. Still, she knew she had to stop. Gathering all her strength, she jerked her head and pulled back.

Breathlessly they looked at each other. Words failed. She shook her head, then reached up and touched her lips swollen with the passion of their kiss. "Oh, my God, what was that?"

"A kiss," he said softly and just as breathlessly, with a smile that made her want to grab him and do it all over again.

Shauna shook her head steadily. "No, no, what was that? What was I thinking? I can't believe I just kissed you," she said to herself. "Dr. Coles, I'm…" she began, still shaking her head in disbelief.

"Perhaps under the circumstances you'd better call me Dominik," he said, smiling broadly.

"I'm so sorry about this. That was totally unprofessional. I don't know what came over me."

"Shauna—I may call you Shauna now—if you hadn't noticed, I'm not complaining," he said softly.

"You don't understand. I've never done anything like this before. It was a reckless disregard for protocol."

"Correction, it was a kiss, a very nice kiss, actually."

"Oh, my God, you could be married with five kids and…"

"Shauna, relax. I don't have a wife and I don't have any children and I gather neither do you."

She continued to shake her head. "No. I have to get someone else to do this review now. I compromised everything—my ethics, my professionalism, my principles, my…"

"Shauna," he interrupted, taking her hands, "it was a kiss. We just got caught up in impulse, the heat of the moment."

"I don't do impulse and my impartiality has been tainted."

"Listen to me, it was a physical need. We both felt it and we both enjoyed it. Are you saying you're unable to separate your professional life from your personal life? You can't have a purely physical need satisfied without compromising your professional ethics?"

"Yes, of course I can. It's just that…"

"What?" he asked.

She stared at him. She knew he was right. She could separate her personal feelings from her job. She'd already done it by coming here. "Yes, of course I can," she relented again.

He nodded. "Good. Then I suggest we move on, unless of course you'd prefer to kiss me again, because if you do…" He stepped closer to her.

She gasped. A scant instant later, the office door opened and Dr. Gilman came in. Shauna and Dominik looked at her as if they'd been caught with their hands in the cookie jar. Dr. Gilman looked at the two of them, then focused on Dominik. Her brow furrowed in warning. "Am I interrupting something?" she asked.

Dominik smiled, being overly charming as he picked up the papers that fell on the floor the second time. "No, not at all, Dr. Gilman. Ms. Banks and I were just discussing professional ethics and its emotional place in our respective professions. A few papers fell off the desk."

"Really?" Dr. Gilman said.

"I have to go. Thank you, Dr. Gilman, for seeing me. I appreciate your time. If you could find me a quiet place to work for the next few weeks, I'd be grateful."

"Yes, the first-floor conference room would be perfect. I'll have the boxes and files delivered there first thing Monday morning. Dominik can show you when he takes you around this evening."

"No, that won't be necessary," she said abruptly.

"But, Ms. Banks, what about your tour of the E.R. this evening?" Dr. Gilman said. "Didn't you want see it today?"

"Actually, I'm running late for another appointment. I'll see the conference room and the E.R. department Monday morning, if that's okay with you, everyone," she said, deliberately not looking at Dominik the whole time.

"Sure, no problem," Dr. Gilman said, then looked at Dominik.

"I'm available for you at any time," Dominik said eagerly.

"Good. So, thank you for seeing me today, Dr. Gilman, Dr. Coles," Shauna said as she grabbed her jacket and briefcase. "Have a good weekend." She walked out quickly and hurried to the elevator. As soon as she pressed the button, the doors opened. She got in and pressed the button to the lobby repeatedly. When the doors closed, she she took a deep breath and watched the red numbers descend. When the doors opened again, she hurried out to her car, blasted the air conditioner and drove off.

Her heart was still pounding like a jackhammer when she stopped at the first traffic light. She glanced up at her reflection in the rearview mirror. She looked the same, she felt the same, but she knew she wasn't. "That was stupid," she chastised herself, openly banging her fist on the steering wheel. She shook her head in complete disbelief. "What were you thinking? You kissed him. This isn't high school."

She was headed to the hotel, intending to change clothes, when she realized it was later than she thought. Dinner with Pearl was at seven, so she turned toward town to find the bakery Pearl mentioned. What she needed to do now was exactly what Dominik said— move on. She stopped at a small specialty food store and bought two bottles of wine and got directions to Nikita's Café. It was on the next block.

As soon as she crossed the threshold of the bakery, she relaxed. The smells permeating the café were heavenly. She chose a number of small sample desserts and had them boxed. Feeling much better, she drove to her old neighborhood. She knew she had to go back to the E.R., back to him, but not right now. Everything was fine for right now.

Chapter 5

"That was odd. All right, what was all that?" Dr. Gilman asked.

"What was all what?" Dominik asked innocently.

"You know exactly what I'm talking about," she said, walking around to the back of her desk and scanning his face the whole time. "Shauna Banks ran out of here like her tail was on fire. What happened?"

"Nothing happened. Seriously, nothing of note happened."

"Of note," she stipulated and repeated. "Elaborate anyway."

"Ms. Banks and I were talking and she accidently placed her hand on the files on the desk. They fell all over the floor. I helped her pick them up and that was just about it."

"You didn't upset her or tell her your feelings about the Cura Group and the buyout?"

"I might have mentioned it," Dominik said.

Dr. Gilman shook her head. "If you weren't the best damn doctor in this medical center, I'd…" She shook her head, not finishing the sentence.

Dominik laughed. They both knew she'd never get rid of him. He was way too valuable of a medical professional and a community leader. He drew nothing but positive attention to the center and to her as the administrator. "Everything will be fine. Trust me." He winked and backed up toward the office door.

"Get out," she said jokingly, drily. "Carry on and have a good weekend."

Dominik left Gilman's office still chuckling. He headed back down to the E.R. He quickly assembled and met with his evening staff, then went back to his office. As soon as he sat down, he reached up and touched his lips.

The kiss was definitely unexpected but most certainly enjoyed. He knew they both wanted more, and given the slightest provocation, there was no telling where they might have taken it. The thought of their making love in an unlocked office excited him. He had never been one for reckless behavior; he usually left that to his older brother, Mikhail. But there was something about Shauna that made him want to open her up and taste the rewards.

Perhaps it was her seemingly closed mind or the sexy body and stunning eyes or maybe her perfectly fitted clothing juxtaposed with her no-nonsense attitude. Whatever it was, he made up his mind that he wanted more. There was a tigress beneath all that prim-and-proper work ethic, and releasing her would be an interesting, not to mention enjoyable, challenge. He was always up for a challenge. He smiled.

There was a knock on the door. His assistant had left for the day and because he'd just spoken to his staff, he doubted it was one of them. He smiled as a stray thought crossed his mind—Shauna Banks. Perhaps he'd have the opportunity to start his little challenge right now. It would be just like her to show up unannounced. He stood up, crossed the room and opened the door.

His brother stood at the door smiling. "Hey."

The expression on Dominik's face was far less than thrilled to see him. "Hey, come on in," Dominik said as he turned and headed back to his desk. He sat down and looked at the computer monitor and then began typing. "I'll be ready in ten minutes. I just have to finish up a few things."

Mikhail strolled in after his brother and took a seat. "No problem. So, who were you expecting?" Mikhail asked.

"What? No one. Why?" Dominik said, answering an email and reading through the daily E.R. medical report.

"Well, because the deliriously happy smile on your face turned around as soon as you saw it was me at the door. Ergo, you were expecting someone else—a woman, I'd gather."

"Yeah, I guess I was, kind of." He shook his head. His brother was good. Most times he'd put both Sherlock Holmes and Watson to shame. The scary part was that deduction and reason were the least of his many talents. "It's this woman. I don't know what kind of game she's playing, but I swear she's getting to me."

"What do you mean?"

"She comes into the E.R. at five o'clock this morning and sits in the waiting room talking to one of the patients about the staff. She's dressed in jeans and a top with a baseball cap on. I thought she was a reporter, so I toss her butt out. The next time I see her, it's hours later and she's back in the E.R. waiting room. This time she's totally professional, wearing a dress and heels. Then later Gilman calls me up to her office and she's in there waiting for me. She works for the Cura Medical Group."

"You mean the company trying to buy the hospital?" Mikhail asked.

"Yeah, she works for them as a consultant. Her job is to check us out and perhaps make the final decision."

Mikhail shrugged. "Reconnaisance. It's all good. It's not like we're talking Harris Bowman. You've turned the E.R. department completely around one hundred percent in just a few months."

"Yeah, I know. The department is on point. That's not the thing. So, we're alone in Gilman's office and we're discussing the Cura Group, and she's trying to defend them when she turns around and knocks some files off the desk. We pick them up and she kisses me."

Mikhail laughed out loud. "She what?" he said.

"Yeah, you heard me. She kissed me."

"Whoa, I did not see that coming. I like it—unpredictable."

"And I'm not talking about some 'thanks for helping me pick up the papers' peck on the cheek. I'm talking about a full-frontal, hot-and-heavy, about-to-clear-the-desk-and-throw-down-serious-lip-locking kiss till the end kiss. Bro, I gotta tell you, she took me completely by surprise. I had no idea it was coming. And I gotta say she had me one hundred percent."

Mikhail continued chuckling. "Well, it's about time you get out of that self-imposed celibate groove you've been in lately."

"I'm not in a celibate groove. I'm selective and you know I've been too busy for all the drama. And truthfully, the women I've been meeting lately are just too clingy. They want all or nothing right up front. You gotta put a ring on their finger on the first date. I can't do that."

"You know it's the doctor title that gets them, don't you? So, I hope you locked the office door and got busy."

"Nah, nothing happened. But afterward she was stunned. For real, I could see it in her face. And I swear she was furious with herself, and she apologized to me."

Mikhail shook his head. "Bro, you got me. I'm good, but I'm the last person to try to figure out women."

"Yeah, but the thing is, there's something about her, just like before. I'm intrigued."

"What do you mean, 'just like before'?" Mikhail asked.

Dominik smiled. "There's no way I'd forget her. We went to school together."

"College or med school?"

"High school, Key West High, to be exact."

"What? When?" Mikhail asked.

"You had already graduated when she came. And it was only for junior and senior years. We graduated and then she just disappeared. She didn't have any real friends, so I never knew what happened to her, but I was always curious." He smiled.

"Sounds like you had a little crush on her."

"I'm not gonna lie—I had something. She was fine and now she's stunning. I don't know if it was a crush or what, but I remember her."

"Does she know you remember her?"

"No, and I'm gonna let her have her moment. Like I said, I don't know what kind of game she's playing, but that kiss definitely said something."

"Hell, yeah, of course it did. You've been challenged. The gauntlet has been thrown down. Now, I'm not saying she was teasing you or playing you, 'cause it doesn't sound like that was the case. The fact that she was stunned with her own actions and apologized to you says something. But still, something prompted her action and your response. I think it only fitting you explore the possibilities."

"Words of wisdom?" Dominik asked his brother.

"Yes, of course, that and treasure every minute you have. Each is special and will never come again. Carpe diem, seize the day."

"That's pretty deep. Anything I should know about, Mikhail?"

"Nah, nothing," he shook his head. "Just like you said, words of wisdom."

Dominik knew his brother held secrets pertaining to his job and he never pressed him, but they both knew they could count on each other no matter what. He turned off his desktop and stored his laptop in his briefcase, then placed it in a locked drawer. "You ready to go?"

Mikhail nodded. "Yeah, let's do it," he said, then stood and headed to the door. "I'll drive, then drop you off back here. Everybody's showing up, so parking is going to be a pain."

"All right," Dominik said as he nodded and waved to several E.R. staff as they passed. He stopped to speak with one of the nurses and then a doctor afterward as they continued out through the security doors.

"What time are you coming in tomorrow morning?"

"I'm not. I'm off tomorrow and Sunday."

"Wow, that's a first. The whole weekend. Any plans?"

"Yeah, but I'll be at the clinic all day tomorrow, and Sunday I'm gonna sleep."

Mikhail chuckled knowing his brother would more than likely be at the clinic all day both days. "Yeah, we'll see how that works out for you. So, what's she like?"

Dominik glanced at Mikhail, then understood. "Opinionated, callous, arrogant," Dominik said.

"Is she attractive?" Mikhail asked. Dominik nodded. "Very attractive?" Mikhail asked again.

"Yes, very attractive."

"Perhaps I'd better check her out for you."

"Nah, you sit this one out," Dominik said.

Mikhail chuckled. "All right. So, what's her name?"

"Shauna Banks."

"Does she live in Key West?"

"The Cura Group is out of D.C., so I presume she's from that area, or maybe Maryland or Virginia," Dominik said as he and his brother walked through the parking lot to Mikhail's car.

Twenty minutes later, the front door opened as they walked up the path. Mia Morales, their cousin's very pregnant wife, stood waiting. "Hey, you made it," she said, smiling happily.

"Yeah, sorry we're late," Dominik said. "How are you feeling?"

"I feel fat and happy," Mia said, hugging and kissing him.

"Ah, but you look gorgeous," Mikhail said, kissing her cheek while giving her a hug.

"I totally agree," Dominik said.

"You guys are so sweet. And thank you so much for

helping out. We really appreciate it. Tonight is the only time we could get everyone together. Spencer is about to go in the studio, Chase and Nikita are headed to Alaska in a few days, and David's got to make the junket rounds for his new movie. Natalia and the boys are going with him this time."

"Hey, it's our pleasure," Mikhail said. "So, where is everybody, upstairs already?"

"No, we decided to eat first," Mia said, tucking herself between her two cousins and escorting them down the hall to the back of the house. "Everyone's out on the deck."

"Great, I'm starved," Mikhail said, smelling the aroma of grilled meat.

"Mmm, something smells fantastic," Dominik said as they neared the kitchen. "Who cooked?"

"Everybody," Mia said. "Nikita and I prepped the food, then Spencer and Chase manned the grill. Natalia and David did the vegetables, and Tatiana supervised. Then of course we all changed places fifteen minutes later."

Dominik and Mikhail laughed. "Yep, that sounds about right," Mikhail said as they stepped out onto the deck. There was a loud, resounding "Hey!" from the family. Hugs, kisses and handshakes were exchanged. Three hours later, the once-empty room beside Mia and Stephen's bedroom was painted, wallpapered, polished, furnished and decorated. It was the picture-perfect nursery.

After his brother dropped him off, Dominik went back to the hospital. The first person he saw in the E.R. waiting room was a woman in jeans and a baseball cap with her head lowered reading a book. He walked over. "Good evening." She looked up. "I'm sorry. I thought you were someone else."

He walked away and went to his office. He sat down thinking about the evening with his family. His sisters and his cousin looked so happy that he couldn't help but think about his own life and his future happiness. He'd always wanted a family and children, but his profession required his steadfast dedication to his field. The rewards were heartwarming when he saw a child's sparkling smile or a patient overjoyed with good news, but the solitude it entailed was lonely. He knew he wanted more. He needed more.

He stood, grabbed his briefcase from the drawer and checked in with the night-shift medical team quickly, then headed back out to the front. As he passed through the waiting room, he looked around once more, this time seeing a sight that made him smile. Shauna was standing at the security desk and speaking with one of the guards. Perfect.

Chapter 6

After the fiasco in Dr. Gilman's office, Shauna drove to her old neighborhood and down her old street. Here, the tropical laissez-faire lifestyle was at its best. She parked in Pearl's driveway behind her car. She got out, grabbed the wine and dessert box, and headed up the brick path to the front door. She looked up at the grand old Victorian home with its wraparound veranda and lush, verdant gardens. As soon as she stepped up onto the open porch, Pearl opened the door smiling with a huge hug for her. "Oh, my God, look at you. I don't care what they say, that Skype is nothing compared to real life. You look sensational. Come on in," Pearl said, overjoyed to see her.

Shauna couldn't stop smiling as she walked in. Pearl

always knew how to make her feel great even if she didn't know she was doing it. "Thank you, Pearl, and you look sensational. You lost weight and look great. I love your hair like that."

"Me, too," Pearl said, reaching up and pressing down the short, curly hair cut Afro-style in the back. "I got so tired of washing that longer hair, so I had it all cut off. Then I decided to just let the gray come in. Dyeing it and rinsing it every other week is nonsense. So, I've gone natural and it feels fabulous." She shook her head and flipped pretend hair over her shoulder.

They laughed. "I know I'm a little bit early, but I couldn't wait to see you." They hugged again. "Hmm, something smells incredible. I stopped and grabbed wine and dessert."

"Perfect and perfect," Pearl said, smiling. "Come on into the kitchen. I'm just finishing up dinner."

"What are we having?" Shauna asked.

"All your favorites," Pearl said.

Shauna hugged her again. "Thank you, Pearl. I really needed to see a friendly face right now."

Pearl looked at her and nodded. "You've got that and all the love you can hold in your heart. Now, never mind about your day right now. We'll talk about what's troubling you in a minute. Right now, go upstairs and wash your hands and get ready to eat."

Shauna nodded and did exactly as she was told. When she returned to the kitchen, everything was ready, but Pearl wasn't there. Shauna heard her humming out on the back deck. She walked over and stood at the screened door. Candle lanterns hung from the deck's wooden beams and the joyous sound of wind chimes played music as the summer breeze blew.

"It's so beautiful here," she said softly. She stepped outside and glanced at the house next door, her house. It was where she'd grown up. It was still very large but it looked different now. The trees were cut and trimmed shorter, the white siding she remembered was now tan, matching the new roof. The playhouse she'd helped build with her mother and father was gone and a gazebo was in its place. She sighed thinking, *If only...*

Pearl stepped up and placed her hand on her shoulder. "They're nice people with two sons and a daughter. They love the home very much."

Shauna nodded. "I'm glad." She looked out at the well-lit backyard garden with its fragrant, colorful flowers, large swimming pool, tall palm tree and privacy shrubs. "I always loved it here. When you took me in after mom died, I..." she began but stopped and took a deep breath.

"You know I have plenty of room here still. There's no one but me. Why don't you go back to the hotel, get your things and then come stay with me? I'd love the company, and think of the money you'll save."

"Thank you, Pearl. The Cura Group is putting me up, but I'll tell you what, after I finish this job I'll hang around the city a few more days. We can catch up."

Pearl smiled happily. "Yes, that sounds wonderful.

I can think of a dozen things we can do. It'll be like a mini vacation."

Shauna nodded. "I could use a mini vacation."

"Good. Now come on. Let's eat before the food gets cold."

Shauna nodded and followed Pearl back inside. Lids came off pots and pans. Pearl had prepared a feast. They made their plates and went back outside on the screened-in deck to eat. By the time they finished eating, it was sunset and everything had been perfect. They each drank a glass of wine with dinner and sipped on sweetened sassafras tea with dessert.

"God, I forgot how wonderful it is to just sit and watch the sunset over the bay."

"You need to slow down. Life isn't a sprint—it's a journey. Forget about chasing the hare, and take it easy and follow the tortoise. Too fast and you miss the best parts. To tell you the truth, I wish I had taken my own advice years ago. I wanted to be at the top of my field and I was for a very long time. I gave up family, surrendered relationships and passed on the love of my life just to be on top. Now retired, I look around and see my past mistake was traveling this journey by myself. Being alone is no fun."

"You have me," Shauna said as she leaned forward, reaching across the table and squeezing her hand softly.

"Yes, I do, and I need you to have someone."

Shauna sat back in her seat and exhaled. "Pearl, I blew the job today." The words tumbled out of her mouth before she realized she was going to say them. "I messed up big-time," Shauna said.

"What do you mean? What happened?" Pearl said.

"Truthfully, I have no idea. Talk about unethical. I can't believe I just completely destroyed all of my credibility. One minute I'm picking papers off the floor and the next I had my tongue in his mouth."

"Whoa, whoa, whoa, back up. Who are we talking about? You had your tongue in whose mouth? Start from the beginning and talk slowly. What happened exactly?"

Shauna told Pearl about her encounter with Dr. Coles, but she was more interested in the hospital.

"Dr. Dominik Coles thinks the Cura Group is gonna buy the hospital and then sell it off to eventually close down?" Pearl asked.

Shauna looked her friend in the eye. "I don't know. I hope not, but I can't guarantee they won't."

"So, he may have legitimate concerns."

"Yes. They sold the last three medical facilities they bought, and within months they began to fail miserably. They resold and eventually the facilities closed."

"Three hospitals closed down?" Pearl said, astonished.

"No," Shauna said, "one small hospital and two medical clinics. They all had major problems. I rejected them all, but the new CEO bought them anyway. At first I couldn't see the sense in it. Then I saw the bottom line. They made more money gutting and then reselling."

Pearl shook her head. "That's absolutely unthinkable."

Shauna nodded. "I agree, but there was nothing I could do. There's a new executive director. His name is Simon Patterson. The bottom line is all he sees. The Cura Medical Group you knew years ago is gone. It's all about making money for the shareholders now. The medical element is out of the picture. Their methods are reprehensible."

"Are you going to stay with them?"

"No. My contract is up and this is my last assignment."

"What about the other company, Relso Health Care?"

"They're completely different. They actually care about the companies they buy. They'd be a much better fit to purchase the medical center."

"Can't you hook them up together?"

"No, on this I'm still under contract with Cura. If they release me, I'm free to offer my services elsewhere."

"Okay, getting back to what you were saying before, what happened with Dr. Coles?" Pearl asked.

Shauna nodded. "Years ago we went to high school together. I had a crush on him—every girl in school did. He was the guy most likely to succeed at everything and I was the girl whose father just embezzled money and ran away with another woman, leaving his sick wife and daughter with divorce papers on the dining room table."

"Shauna, what your father did was heinous. He was greedy and selfish and he lied to everybody, but that was his failing, not yours," Pearl said adamantly.

"Yes, I know," Shauna said softly. "I left this place

fifteen years ago and never looked back. Now, coming back here brings back so many memories. Most of them aren't so good. My mom died in Key West Medical. I took her there thinking they'd help her. She never walked out."

"Shauna, your mother was sick and no one knew it. Ovarian cancer has no real symptoms and is nearly impossible to diagnose. By the time we all found out, it was just too late."

"I should have paid more attention to her after Dad left us."

"What happened was nobody's fault, certainly not yours. No one knew, not even her until it was too late. It was misdiagnosed. Now, what happened today? What makes you think you blew the account?"

"I guess I just didn't expect to see Dominik. It's crazy. It feels like being seventeen all over again. It's like the universe is messing with me again."

"Okay, now you're sounding a little paranoid. Tell me what happened after you kissed him. What did he say?"

"Nothing really. He was okay about it. He was understanding and even charming. He said what happened was just a physical impulse—the heat of the discussion—and that we should be able to distance ourselves and move on and continue doing our jobs."

"He's right, and you can do that. You do it every time you walk into a hospital or medical office. You leave your emotions outside. It's your job to be objective and remove the emotional element from the situation, and you're very good at it, right?"

Shauna nodded. "Yes."

"Okay, then it's all good, business as usual. You'll just pretend like it never happened, right?"

Shauna took a deep breath. "Right," she said, agreeing with relief.

"Except one last thing—how was he?" Pearl smiled eagerly.

"You did not just ask me that question," Shauna said.

"Come on, spill. I know exactly who you're talking about. We've met on a few occasions. He's a very intense man with a quiet and powerful presence. When he and his brother walk into a room, the women can't help but stare. He's a puzzle, though. I've never been able to see through his armor. It's interesting to know that you've at least glimpsed a crack in it."

"What do you mean?"

"I mean Dr. Coles is built and he's gorgeous and as sexy as hell. And it's a good thing I'm not a cougar or I'd go after him myself. And let's face it, Shauna, you haven't had a hookup in about three years. You're due for a little L and L."

"What are 'L and L'?"

"Lust and love," she said. "So, let's hear details."

"Seriously, I cannot believe you're asking me this. It was just a kiss. It was quick and over with," she said. She looked at Pearl, who was steadily shaking her head, not believing a word. "Okay, okay, it was without words. I swear my heart stopped beating the whole time. My toes curled and I wanted it to go on forever."

Pearl nodded. "That's more like it."

"And that said, I'm gonna end this conversation and grab some more dessert before I head back to the hotel." Shauna stood to go back inside.

"You know, I was just thinking," Pearl began as she followed behind Shauna, "while you're down here, and seeing as how you know the good doctor and haven't had your toes curled since the turn of the last century, why don't you and he…"

"Do not finish that sentence," Shauna warned jokingly.

Pearl laughed. "It was only a thought, a hopeful suggestion. Are you going back to the E.R. tonight?"

"I don't know. Probably. I don't want to go back, but I know I have to. I don't have a choice."

"You're right. You do have to go back. It's your job and you can do this," Pearl said. "Get yourself right back up on the horse. That's what I like to hear. And speaking of going back, I presume you received your Key West High School alumni emailed newsletter?"

Shauna shrugged and nodded. "I unsubscribed years ago, but it still comes and goes directly to my spam filter."

Pearl shook her head. "Well, you need to get it out of the spam filter and read it. Your class is having a high school reunion in two weeks. I hear it's gonna be nice."

"Yeah, I heard."

"As long as you're gonna still be here, why don't you think of attending this year? You didn't go to your prom. You haven't been back in fifteen years. It might be a nice evening out. So, what do you have planned for tomorrow?" Pearl asked Shauna, completely changing the subject.

"Nothing much. I'll get some work done, of course."

"Nonsense, you can work Monday. See, that was my big mistake—I worked all the time. My life just passed me by and all I did was work. Then what are you left with? Nothing. Tomorrow you can come volunteering with me. And don't give me that 'I don't have time.' You make time."

Shauna smiled. "Volunteering. What kind of volunteering? Do you mean feeding the hungry?"

"There are all kinds of volunteering with so many in need and never enough people to help out. I usually put in hours with the senior citizens at the center, but tomorrow I'll be hanging out with a couple of dear old ladies."

"Okay, what do I have to do?" Shauna asked.

"Nothing much. Just smile, be pleasant, help them in and out of the car and with their purchases. Most seniors don't drive, so going to the store, going out to run errands or to the clinic is a major hardship. They have no way to get around. That's where I come in."

"So, you just play chauffeur all day."

"Sometimes, but it's mainly just being there with them. Most of them are alone. They don't have any family, or if they do, they don't see them much."

Shauna nodded. It sounded good. She always wanted to volunteer but never found she had time. Pearl was right. You don't find time—you make time. "Okay, that sounds great. I'll do it."

"Good."

"Good," Shauna repeated. Then they laughed and Pearl began telling her about the books she'd downloaded and the one she was currently reading. Shauna responded and commented when necessary, but her mind was on Pearl's last comment about Dominik. It would be tempting to finally fulfill her teenage fantasy of being with him. She smiled to herself. Never in a million years would she have guessed her day would end like this.

Later that evening, after long hugs goodbye, Shauna went back to the hotel. It had been an arduous day, but still she was wide-awake. She didn't want to go back to the hotel room and be alone, but she did. Pearl was right—being alone was the worst.

She sat down at the small desk and pulled out her computer pad and laptop. She transferred updates and synchronized the data between computers. She preferred to work primarily on her laptop for the majority of her work, but used her lighter computer tablet for taking notes and general information gathering.

Now that the laptop was up-to-date, she reached into her briefcase to get her flash drives. She pulled one out, then opened the case wider to retrieve the second one. It wasn't there. She started digging and rifling through each compartment more thoroughly, pulling everything out. The case was completely empty. She looked again and again. She grabbed the case and nearly turned it inside out. Then she stopped and looked around the empty room. "Oh, no, this isn't happening," she muttered to herself.

The missing drive, although password protected, had a number of very sensitive files on it that related to her work and the Cura Group. Losing that flash drive wouldn't hinder her job or performance, but it would make it take longer. And even though the same basic program was also on her laptop, she'd already begun singling out specific files to be examined more closely. She'd have to do that part all over again.

She had to find it. She began searching her briefcase again and then her purse and her suitcase. It was nowhere in sight. She sat down on the side of the bed and tried to remember the last time she used it. It was at her last job, but she knew she had it when she came here. Then it hit her. It might have fallen out when she dropped her briefcase on the floor in the E.R. waiting area earlier that morning. She needed to go back to the E.R. She grabbed her purse and keys and hurried out to the car.

Leaving anything behind was a huge misstep, something she'd never done. Leaving a very key component of her job because she was mesmerized by Dominik looking at her was an unforgivable breach in conduct. She'd never been so reckless before. She never allowed her emotions to get in the way of her job or get the best of her. But once was already once too many times. She knew she'd have to shield and protect herself more than ever now.

Chapter 7

There were only a few people waiting in the open area. This wasn't about checking out the staff and procedures. Shauna stepped up to the nurse's check-in desk. "Hi, I lost something here earlier. Is there someone I can speak with?"

"Sure. I'll call for security."

"It was this morning. Maybe housekeeping picked it up?"

"If they did, it still has to be handled through security."

Shauna nodded, hoping that the same guards who'd escorted her out earlier weren't on duty this evening. She was dressed in the same outfit and heels from this afternoon. Still, it was possible they could confuse her for a reporter again. A few minutes later a guard came out through the security doors. He was thin and tall, well over six feet and probably weighed no more than one hundred pounds. "Hi, can I help you?" he asked.

"Yes, I hope so. I was here earlier this morning and I think I accidently dropped a flash drive on the floor in the waiting room. Did anyone turn it in?"

The guard shook his head. "Not to my knowledge. If they did, it would be in Lost and Found, but it's closed right now. You can come back Monday morning at nine o'clock."

Shauna frowned. This wasn't good enough. She needed that flash drive. "Okay, here's the thing. I need the flash drive tonight and this weekend. Is there any way you can just check? It's really important."

"Sorry, I wish I could help. That's hospital policy. Lost and Found is in the hospital-services department. Their department's closed on the weekends. No one gets in after hours. It's for security."

Shauna understood, of course, but that didn't make it any easier for her. "Well, what if something is found in the middle of the night, like right now? Where does it go?"

"We hold it here in the back until the Lost and Found opens."

"Can you check to see if someone turned in a flash drive?"

"Yeah, sure, I can do that," he said. "I'll check the

daily write-up reports, as well. Flash drives would fall into the expensive and secure item category."

"Thank you so much," she said.

He disappeared through the security doors. Shauna waited impatiently a few minutes, then she glanced at her watch. It was just before midnight. She looked around the waiting area and decided to walk over and check herself. No one was sitting in the chair she'd sat in earlier that morning. She looked under, around and behind the seats, then moved the cushion. She went back to the security desk just as the guard was returning. He shook his head. "Sorry, ma'am. We have sunglasses, a book and a kid's toy. No flash drive."

"Okay, thanks," Shauna said, obviously disappointed.

"No problem. Check back Monday morning at nine o'clock. Have a good night." He paused, then spoke again. "See ya, Doc. Have a good night."

Shauna turned around. Dominik was standing right behind her. She looked surprised and then looked away, shaking her head.

He smiled at her and then glanced up and answered the security guard. "Thanks, Rodney. You have a good night, too." Then he focused his attention on Shauna. "Good morning, Ms. Banks."

She glanced at the clock above the check-in desk. He was right. It was exactly midnight. "Good morning, Dr. Coles."

"So, am I going to find you hanging out here most nights?"

"No, not anymore."

"Don't tell me you're not going to be spying on us anymore."

"I don't spy," she said quickly. "And as I said, I won't be doing that anymore."

He looked at her and could tell that she was serious. Apparently she meant it when she said she intended to excuse herself from continuing the job. "You're dropping the job. I told you the kiss was…"

She looked at him sharply. "That's not what I meant," she said, lowering her voice and moving closer to him.

"What do you mean?" he asked, enjoying her sweet perfumed skin. This was the scent he remembered from before. It was floral and intoxicating. He realized he hadn't gotten enough.

"I believe my cover has been blown. I think I've been found out. The whole idea of coming here on off-hours was to be inconspicuous, to blend in and watch how the staff works in real situations. I have a feeling that's not going to work anymore." She looked over at the check-in desk, noticing the nurse and security guard watching them intently. The broad smile on their faces and the whispers between them told her coming here to observe wasn't going to be as easy as before.

Dominik followed her line of vision. "Yeah, I guess you have at that. So, what happens now?"

"Now I go to work as planned. The documents and files requested from Cura have been pulled. Monday morning I get to go through them to find out if this hospital is a viable institution worth pursuing financially."

He shook his head. "That's pretty cold. In other words, you're here to find out if this place is a viable commodity. Of course it's viable. We're a hospital. We service the public. The Cura Medical Group doesn't have a clue about what's involved in running this place. It's all about the bottom line for them and for you. You're the typical corporate raider—cold, emotionless, compassionless, with a massive chip on your shoulder. There's no way you're gonna judge this hospital fairly. You see numbers and spreadsheets, not people."

"You make a lot of speeches, but as usual you forgot the facts. Someone needs to look at the bottom line. Obviously no one here has. That's why the place is a mess," she said. "In medical terms, this place is hemorrhaging money. My job is to find the weaknesses and develop workable solutions."

"Even if it means closing it down," he said. She didn't respond. Dominik shook his head. "Question—what about the people who do need us? Do you know how many people need this medical center to be open? How many walk through these doors every day? Do you have a clue how many patients we've treated and saved here?"

"I know one patient you didn't," she snapped quickly. It was pure emotion and it instantly stopped them both.

He looked at her. His eyes narrowed. "What exactly does that mean?" he asked pointedly.

She shook her head. The kiss was bad enough, but to

imply that she knew someone who died at the medical center was a huge mistake. Of course he picked up on it. "This is getting to be a habit, isn't it?"

"What?"

"You and I arguing constantly, like oil and water."

"Yeah, I guess so. Do you want to answer my question now? What exactly does that comment mean?"

Shauna took a deep breath and looked away. The intensity of his stare made her insides sizzle and burn. "Meaning, I do know. I know exactly how many patients come here every day. It's my job to know. Cura did the audit and I read the report."

"No, that was a personal comment," he quickly surmised.

"I have no idea what you're talking about," she said, stepping back. "At this point of my review, I'll be focusing on the E.R. department. Because Dr. Bowman's records are spotty, to say the least, I'll need your assistance to wade through them and get a basic understanding of his procedures. If you can..."

He shook his head. "Who died here?" he asked.

She ignored his questions. "I'll probably have some questions for you. Dr. Gilman said that you'd be my contact, so to speak."

He nodded. "No problem. It will be my pleasure. I'll be available anytime you want me. Did you want me tonight?" he asked. His voice softened seductively.

She looked at him. The question was innocent enough, but she knew it was loaded with sexual innuendo. And she had a feeling he knew it, even though his expression was innocent. "No, not right now. So, I'll see you Monday morning." She turned to walk out.

"Wait, I'm headed out, too. I'll walk you to your car. Safety first."

"That's not necessary," she said, knowing he was going to anyway. She was right. He didn't respond. He just stepped up to walk by her side. As they passed the check-in desk, both the nurse and security guard said good-night.

Shauna had been in enough hospitals and medical centers to know that the rumors would be flying as soon as the sliding glass doors closed behind them. Hospital rumors usually spread faster than germs. And unlike germs, they were seldom, if ever, completely eradicated.

"You know they're gonna talk," she said.

"Nah, of course not. Not at all."

She glanced at him, not sure if he was being naive or facetious. They stepped outside into the hot, muggy night air. The sweltering heat was a stark contrast to the air-conditioned waiting room. "How long will this take?" Dominik asked.

"Two weeks, maybe three or more," she said.

"And you decide the final evaluation?"

"My job is just a small piece of the whole process."

"But a very important piece, I would gather. If you fail us, then the buyout doesn't go through. Am I right?"

"You're giving me too much credit."

"Somehow I don't think I'm giving you enough. Everything was ready to go with the Cura Group and then they brought you in. I presume for your final approval."

"Interesting thought."

"You do that well," he said. She looked over at him questioningly. "Not answering any of my questions."

She chuckled. "Most people don't realize that."

"I'm not most people," he said.

"Yes, I know. I remember."

"There it is again—the subtle innuendo. Do we know each other?" he asked.

"No. I can honestly answer that we do not know each other."

"Did we and I don't remember?" he specified while smiling.

"I'm sure your memory is better than that."

"And again you didn't answer the question."

They got to her rental car and she clicked the key to unlock the driver's side door. "Well, this is me," she said, then turned and looked up into his dark, sexy eyes. The muted lights around them were just enough to make her body begin to sizzle again. "Thanks for walking me to my car."

"Have you eaten yet?"

"Yes, I ate earlier."

"Where are you staying?"

"The Key West Gateway Inn," she said.

"I've never stayed there. Is it nice?"

"Yes, it's very nice. I always liked the look of it."

"So, you've been to Key West before."

She hesitated, realizing her error. She was making too many of them. Being with Dominik was obviously knocking her off guard. "Yes, a very long time ago." She tossed her purse onto the passenger seat.

There was a rumbling in the distance and a few raindrops began to fall. He nodded and looked up at the sky. "Looks like we're gonna have some rain and maybe a storm," he said.

Shauna nodded. "Well, I guess this is good-night," she said. "Thanks for walking me. I'll see you Monday."

"Good night." He turned to walk away.

"Dr. Coles," she called out. He turned around and walked a few steps back to her. There was another rumble. This time it was closer. Shauna hesitated, fighting back the urge to surrender to what she really wanted. She shook the fantasy of their bodies pressed together writhing in hot, sweaty sex aside.

Dominik smiled. "My turn," he whispered. Then he kissed her.

This kiss was tender and inviting. As their lips touched, the fire began to burn through her body. Neither raised their hands or arms to embrace; it was only their lips that connected. Touching over and over again, they pressed softly and then firmly, tasting the sweet essences of passion they knew they had indelibly stamped on each other. When the kiss ended, he stepped back and smiled again. "Get some rest," he said.

She nodded. "Good night," she said again.

He nodded. "Good night, Ms. Banks."

Dominik watched her car drive off. He then turned and headed to his own car. He wondered what it would take to open Shauna's hard outer shell and find the woman he knew was inside. She pretended the only thing she cared about was her job and the bottom line, but he knew better. A brief glimpse into her eyes when that man brought his wife, Anna, into the E.R. told him differently. There was a lot more to Shauna Banks and he wanted to crack her shell.

Shauna stopped at the first traffic light and glanced in the rearview mirror, seeing the medical center behind her. She shook her head. This was going to be much harder than she expected, but all she needed to do was control her feelings.

Years ago she'd made herself strong and she learned how to seal her emotions from the outside world. She could do this. And as soon as this job was over, she'd leave Key West for good and never look back.

The rain began to pour. She drove quickly and steadily, getting back to the hotel just before the storm hit.

Chapter 8

Six hours later, Dominik sat straight up in bed and looked around his still-dark bedroom. He reached over and turned on the bedside lamp. His body was drenched and the cotton sheets were entangled with his legs. He got up and took a cold shower but it didn't help much. He remembered the dream completely—every touch, smell, feel and sound of it seemed so real. Now with a fluffy white towel wrapped around his waist, he went out onto the balcony.

Dreams never bothered him much. They were just stray images and thoughts left over from the day that manifested themselves in subconscious, meaningless mental pictures. Most times he didn't even remember them, but when this one had not only sat him straight up in bed, but sent him into a cold shower, he knew to pay attention.

It started with him walking into his office and seeing Shauna sitting at his desk. There were stacks of papers piled up everywhere. She looked up and smiled at him. Then without speaking, she stood, licked her lips and began unbuttoning her suit jacket. When she finished, he could see she wore nothing underneath. His mouth went dry as he stood watching the slow, sultry seduction.

She reached back to unzip her skirt as she walked around to the front of the desk. It dropped to the floor and she kicked it aside. All she wore were dark blue lace panties and her open jacket and high spiked heels. She turned around. The sweet swell of her ample rear made his body tighten and tense. His hands itched to touch and feel her generous brown cheeks. She leaned over, pushed aside a stack of papers. They fell to the floor. With her body still turned away from him and leaning over the desk, she looked back over her shoulder and raked her teeth over her lower lip. This was his invitation to come closer.

He walked over as she turned and sat back on the desk, waiting with her hands gripping the desk's front edge. He reached down and opened her jacket. Two beautiful breasts beckoned to him. He leaned down and licked her nipple. Her areolae were milk-chocolate Hershey's Kisses and he licked and tasted his fill. She gasped but didn't move. He kissed and licked the other nipple, vibrating his tongue just enough to make her body tremble. He ran his fingers over her forehead, down her face and neck, across her chest, and down her arms and hands. Then he whispered to her, "Turn around."

She stood up and turned for him. Seeing the perfect rear in the blue lace panties up close sent a spike of wanton passion through his body. He ran his hands over her shoulders, down her back to her rear. He grasped and caressed each cheek—massaging, rubbing until he couldn't stand it anymore. He quickly removed his clothes and rubbed his naked body against her as she slowly leaned forward over the desk.

His body trembled with desire as he bent down and slowly eased her blue lace panties down her long, luscious legs. She turned and sat back on his desk and spread her legs for him. He cupped the nape of her neck and tilted her head upward. Her lips parted as his tongue plunged deep into her mouth. They kissed. It was madness. Certainly nothing like he had ever experienced. She wrapped her arms around his neck and held him tightly. He slipped his hand down between her legs and touched her wetness. She moaned to express her pleasure as her hips gyrated to his probing strokes. He was hard and thick and they were both ready.

One finger. Two fingers. Three fingers. Then he grabbed his penis and entered her in one firm thrust. Instantly, an explosion of passion. She gasped loudly and screamed his name as she lay back on the desk. He encircled her rock-hard nipples with the palms of his hands and she wiggled and writhed in pleasure. She wrapped her long legs around his waist and he lifted her from the desk, then pressed her up against the side wall. His large hands grabbed her butt cheeks as his pelvis pressed into her over and over again.

The fierce, intense swell of their passion surged higher and higher. Their bodies tensed, tightening with each gyrating thrust. She dug her nails into his shoulder as their unrestrained climaxes approached. They came, climaxing in a blast of mindless rapture. Their bodies tensed and they peaked again. After the third mind-boggling orgasm, their bodies soared on sated bliss.

Memories of the night before and the dream still with him, Dominik went into his home gym and stepped up onto the treadmill climber. He had some excess energy to release and this was the best way he could think to outrun what he was feeling.

An hour later, he got dressed and headed to the medical center. If there was information on Shauna Banks, the hospital records were the best place to find it. As soon as he got to his office, he sat down at his desk and scanned the hospital computer files. As he expected, Shauna's name was there. She was brought into the E.R. fifteen years ago by her mother with a fever and a sore throat. She was treated and released. There was nothing else noted. Then he checked her mother's name. She was listed as deceased.

All other information was in the hospital records room on the lower level. He headed down and requested her file. He signed it out and took it back to his office.

He sat at his desk and read through the file. Her death certificate didn't elaborate on cause of death. It just listed natural causes. He shook his head. It didn't make sense. He read through the next few papers. They didn't list much, either.

"Dominik, what are you doing here? I thought you had the weekend off," Margaret said, pausing in his office doorway.

Dominik looked up. "Yeah, I do. I just needed to find out about a patient."

"I was just in the E.R. Which patient?" she asked.

"No, it was fifteen years ago. It's Shauna Banks's mother. She died here, but there's not a lot listed on the death certificate and the case file has been sealed. I've never seen a patient's file permanently sealed before and certainly not after so much time has passed."

Margaret walked over to his desk. "The only reason a file would still be sealed is because there was some type of legal proceeding surrounding the case and it is still enforced. We have litigation going on now with Dr. Bowman. Several of his cases have been pulled and sealed by the attorneys."

"Why would it still be sealed after fifteen years?"

"It shouldn't be, but it might still be legally protected."

"How do I find out what's in the file?" Dominik asked.

"You don't," Margaret said. "I do." She held her hand out for the file. Dominik closed it and handed it over. "What exactly are you looking for?" she asked.

"That's just it—I don't know. There's something in her eyes that says there's more going on between her and this facility than just a review. This is personal for her. I'd like to know just how personal."

She nodded. "I'll find out. In the meantime, get out of here. The last thing I need is a burned-out doctor because he doesn't know how to take time off."

Dominik stood to leave. "All right, I'm headed out now. I'll see you Monday."

"Carry on," she said with her usual quick wave.

He left and drove east on the Overseas Highway to the Big Coppitt Key, just on the other side of Boca Chica Key. There was a free medical clinic there in desperate need of medical assistance. He volunteered his time every other weekend from seven until noon and it always made him feel good. He drove to the clinic and parked in the small alley beside the building. It was old but not run-down. It was a godsend to many. When he walked through the front door, he saw that four people were already in line waiting for medical assistance. Dominik spoke, then went inside to start his day.

This labor of love had now become the only thing he did related to being a doctor. His position at the hospital was mainly administrative. This gave him the opportunity to be a doctor again. He enjoyed helping people and making a difference in their lives. He went into the main lounge. One of the lead doctors was already there. While they were talking, another doctor came in. They had a short meeting to catch up and then they prepared to start their busy day. Dominik washed his hands, grabbed the first patient file and walked into the exam room.

From morning until noon, his focus was solely on his patients. He cared for the sick, bandaged the wounded and reset broken bones. Thinking about Shauna was the furthest thing from his mind, but every once in a while, she was there—like a dream, his dream. Monday was in two days. He'd see her again and he couldn't wait.

Chapter 9

Saturday morning, Shauna rolled over in bed and stared at the lackluster drapes at the window. Perfectly pleated, they looked like every paisley, plaid, polka-dot, striped print pattern she'd seen in the past five years. Although she lived in Maryland, she was on the road nine months out of the year. She was proud of what she did for a living. She performed a valuable service by keeping hospitals and medical professions accountable to the people they served. But the constant travel was definitely getting to her.

Waking up in a hotel room bed alone promised her no future except more of the same year after year. She glanced at the illuminated numbers on the clock radio beside the bed. It was six o'clock in the morning. Even though the day before had started well before dawn and she'd worked a full day late into the night, she felt well rested. As a matter of fact, she felt fantastic, even energized.

The storm from last night had passed and this was a new day. She felt the need to do something different—to shake her life up. So, instead of going to the hotel gym and hitting the treadmill like she usually did, she decided to go out into the street to run. She showered, dressed and stepped outside. The sun shone brightly and it looked as if it was going to be a great day. She plugged her earbuds into her ears, turned on her music, stretched a few minutes and then headed out.

Remembering the area well, she decided to run inland, away from the usual beachfront and cruise-ship docks more popular with morning runners. The streets were almost empty except for a few other runners, early-morning strollers and shopkeepers.

She headed toward Petronia Street and the Bahama Village area at Whitehead and Truman streets. This was the neighborhood she and her mother lived in for a while after her father left them. It was poor, run-down and primarily black, getting its name from the many original residents hailing from the islands. But now, it looked very different. It was rejuvenated.

What was once a crowded, low-income family neighborhood was now filled with restaurants, boutiques, specialty shops and multiple tourist attractions, and the centerpiece was a large open-air flea market selling everything imaginable. It was still early, so the mass of weekenders and holiday tourists hadn't descended on the area yet.

Relaxed and in complete control, Shauna enjoyed her run and even extended it a few extra blocks. The upbeat music continued to play as she skirted the main area and took a few side streets to get a better flavor of the revitalized village. She slowed her pace and began walking, realizing that twenty blocks away were Front and Duvall streets. She stopped, deciding not to extend her run to the docks. The last thing she wanted was to get caught up in the cruise-ship arrivals. She turned and headed back to the hotel near the Case Marina neighborhood.

Halfway there, a phone call interrupted her music. She stopped, switched over and answered. "Hello," she said, breathing hard.

"Shauna, is that you? It's Pearl. Are you okay?"

"Hey, Pearl. Yeah, I'm just a little winded. I'm out running. What's up?"

"What's up is how soon will you be ready to go?"

"To go where? What do you mean?" she asked between pants.

"To volunteer. We talked about it last night."

"Oh, Pearl, I completely forgot all about that. I've been out running all morning. Maybe you should go without me. I'll catch up with you next time."

"Where are you?" she asked.

"I'm at the Bahama Village, headed back to the hotel."

"Good. Get showered, get changed into something

cool and comfortable. You can pick me up in an hour. I'll be ready."

"An hour. No, there's no way I'll be ready in an hour."

"Sure there is, if you get started now. See you in an hour."

Pearl hung up and Shauna looked around as her music began playing again. She leaned over onto her knees and took a deep breath. She was already exhausted. Now she had to sprint back to the hotel, shower, change and then get over to Pearl's house. She shook her head. She thought about Pearl standing on the porch waiting for her. She couldn't let that happen. She adjusted her earbuds and took off running like the wind.

Fifty-three minutes later, Shauna pulled up in front of Pearl's house. Pearl was out front watering and dead-heading her flowers. She glanced at her watch, smiled and waved as the car pulled into the driveway. "Good morning. Perfect timing."

Shauna got out of the car smiling. "Good morning."

"Now you see what you can do when you really put your mind to it," Pearl said.

"I still can't believe I made it. But we'll need to stop and get me some tea. As a matter of fact, where are we headed?"

"No problem. We're off to pick up a few senior citizens and take them shopping. After that, we'll just hang out." Pearl walked up the front steps to the porch. She locked the front door, grabbed her purse and two cups of tea. She met Shauna at the car with a grin. "You didn't think I forgot you, did you?"

Shauna beamed, knowing better. "No, of course not."

They got in and Pearl handed her the tea. "Thanks," Shauna said, starting the engine. "Where to first?"

"The cemetery," Pearl said.

"The cemetery?" Shauna questioned.

"Yes, the Pennington sisters live nearby—Mae and Wanda Pennington. They're originally from New York. They pooled their money and moved here a few years ago. They couldn't take the cold winters anymore. I usually pick them up on my way over to the seniors' center. But today we're just going to help them shop for a party they're throwing."

"That's nice, two sisters throwing a party together."

"Well, it's a bit more than that. I should warn you, the Pennington sisters aren't exactly your sweet old ladies who knit and bake cookies for the neighborhood kids."

"What do you mean?"

"You'll see," Pearl said.

Moments later they were driving through the city. Although the charm of Key West was its diversity, not everyone enjoyed the good life and the million-dollar homes. Unlike Old Key West with its shops and stylish homes and New Town with its lavish tourist locations, certain sections of the Keys were less appealing. Granted, there were no "bad" neighborhoods in Key West per se—sometimes million-dollar homes were right next to trailers. They drove through Old Town, then continued to the less desirable locations to visit and live, particularly in off hours. "I forgot how bad it looks around here."

"Well, like most major municipalities in tourist cities, there is no known poverty. In other words, the indigent had been tucked away and swept aside. Impoverished and destitute, they had nothing."

"Yeah," Shauna said softly, remembering that feeling well. She and her mother lived that life for a time. They were the forgotten. Pearl pointed and Shauna turned down as small one-way street and pulled up in front of a tiny house with bright red hurricane shutters. An elderly woman waved from the front porch and came right out to the car with her sister close behind.

As soon as Shauna saw them, she smiled. They were exactly as she expected. One wore a print summer dress with a delicate lace collar and the other wore a very dressy skirt and top. They had pure white hair combed in French twists, wore pearl necklaces and carried patent-leather handbags. They smiled sweetly and their eyes sparkled as bright as their red lipstick.

As soon as they got into the car, it livened up. Pearl made introductions and immediately the sisters began their interrogation. They were a tag team of outrageousness. The Pennington sisters were more interested in asking Shauna personal questions than anything else. "But you're young and pretty—why don't you have a man in your life?" Mae Pennington asked.

"It's not that easy out here, ladies," Shauna said hoping that would end their interest in her life.

"Lord, child, when I was your age I was beating them back with a stick. I had just about every man from Buffalo to New Rochelle after me," Wanda Pennington said to a bevy of cackling laughter from Mae.

"That's the absolute truth," Mae insisted, still laughing.

The conversation continued and got even more outrageous as they headed east on Overseas Highway and continued driving past Stock Island. Pearl gave directions and Shauna followed.

"Well, if you don't have a man in your life, what do you do for sex?" Wanda Pennington asked plainly, as if ordering lunch.

Shauna's jaw dropped. She dared not look up into the rearview mirror into the backseat. Instead, she looked over at Pearl, who was giggling with her head turned facing the side window. It was obvious this was nothing new for her.

"You should never neglect your orgasms," Mae warned.

"She's right. All that pent-up pressure ages you," Wanda attested. "Look at us. We're both well over eighty years old and doing just fine. Sex is the secret. So, how much sex do you have, dear?"

Shauna's face burned bright red. She couldn't believe the comments and questions coming out of these ladies' mouths. "Wanda, look, you made her blush," Mae said.

"You can't ask questions like that. Some people are old-fashioned about sex. They don't like to talk about it. Besides, she probably has a few vibrators, like a rabbit or bullet. Isn't that right, Shauna?"

"Well, if she's blushing now, what in the world is she going to do when we go shopping for the party?" Wanda asked. Pearl burst out loud with laughter.

A few minutes later, Pearl pointed for Shauna to pull into a parking space a few doors down from a health clinic. They all got out and walked toward the clinic. Shauna, walking ahead, stopped and opened the clinic's door. But Pearl followed the Pennington sisters, who had continued walking. "No," Pearl said to Shauna, "not there." She walked a few stores farther down the block and stopped, opening the door for the sisters. "Here."

Shauna looked up at the sign. It was an adult toy store. To say she was stunned and mortified was an understatement. "Are you kidding me? What kind of party are they having?"

Pearl laughed. "Your expression is priceless."

Shauna followed them inside. That early in the morning, they were the only customers, so they had free rein of the store's many enticements.

Shauna never considered herself a prude, but she was amazed at all the things she'd never seen before. Of course, the Pennington sisters had, and Pearl, having shopped with them a number of times before, had, as well. They offered to purchase Shauna a few salacious items, but she nicely but very adamantly declined. They browsed and shopped for over an hour, both sisters finally purchasing a large shopping bag of items each with, of course, their seniors' discount.

"Okay, where to now?" Shauna asked, taking the two bags from the counter.

"Shauna, would you take those to the car?" Mae said. "We're gonna check out a few more things. We'll be right out."

"Sure," Shauna said, then opened the door and headed out.

She walked back to the car chuckling to herself. What she'd assumed was going to be an ordinary day had turned out to be anything but. And the two sweet old ladies she expected to meet turned out to be two hot mammas with enough moxie to level a ten-story building. She wondered if she'd have half the pluck the Pennington sisters had at their age. She chuckled again.

"Shauna."

Hearing her name called, she stopped. It was impossible. Still, she knew the voice. It was too deep and too damn sexy to be anyone else. She turned around and saw Dominik coming out of the health clinic. Her eyes widened. He was smiling as he approached. She was speechless, while shaking her head.

"Hey, good morning. This is a surprise. Of all the people to see, you're the last person I expected."

"Um, hi," she said, still stunned to see him.

"So, what are you doing so far away from your computer? I thought you worked nonstop." A slow, easy smile crossed his face. Watching her was definitely a pleasure.

"Believe it or not, I do take time off to relax. But I could say the same of you. I'm surprised you're not at the hospital."

"I actually have a day off."

"And so you hang out here." She looked up at the clinic.

"Yes, I volunteer here at the clinic every other weekend. It's a free clinic for those without health care. Most of the doctors in the area pitch in when they can."

She nodded. "That's good. It's needed."

"Yes, I agree. I saw you walk by and couldn't believe it was you." He looked down. "And I see you've been shopping," he said.

She looked down and saw that she was still holding the shopping bags with the store's very distinct name and logo. One bag had a very recognizable item resembling a replica of a man's penis. "I'm here with some friends," she said, "and it's a long story."

"Really? I'd be interested in hearing it sometime. Perhaps we can get together this evening."

"Um…"

"Shauna," Pearl called out, "a little help."

Shauna and Dominik turned to see Pearl and the Pennington sisters walking toward them with another large bag. Dominik walked over to the ladies as Shauna unlocked the doors and followed. Dominik stepped between the sisters, allowing each to take his arm for balance. "Good morning, ladies," Dominik said.

They smiled blissfully at his chivalry. "Now, you're what I call a real gentleman," Wanda said.

Shauna opened the trunk and began putting the two shopping bags inside. The whole time the Pennington sisters were peppering Dominik with questions.

"A doctor," Mae said, obviously pleased. "How wonderful."

"Where do you work, in private practice?" Wanda asked.

"No, I'm the acting E.R. director at Key West Medical Center."

"Nice, very nice," they both said.

"Shauna, no wonder you didn't want us to buy anything for you. You have the real thing right here."

Shauna cringed and groaned, totally embarrassed. "Ladies, Dr. Coles and I aren't together intimately."

"Well, why not?" Wanda asked.

"Such a waste," Mae added.

"Two single, attractive people who obviously have chemistry shouldn't be wasting time. Get busy."

"I totally agree," Dominik said, looking at Shauna innocently.

She glared at him for encouraging them. She looked to Pearl for assistance, but she was too busy chuckling. "Ladies, Dr. Coles and I are professional colleagues. It would be inappropriate for us to be intimate. We have to work together."

"So?" Wanda said.

"Oh, for heaven's sake," Mae exclaimed, "if every-body felt that way, the human race would have gone ex-tinct a few million years ago. Sex in the workplace is like gossip over coffee. Enjoy it and do it often."

"Exactly. There's absolutely nothing wrong with sex on the job," Wanda added. "As a matter of fact..."

Shauna grabbed Pearl's bag, not wanting to hear any more. As she shoved it into the trunk, the top item dropped out. Dominik picked it up and read the label. It was impossible not to know what it was. Shauna looked away. "Edible panties. Interesting," he said. "I wonder what the nutritional value is."

"Oh, now the surprise is ruined. We got them for you, Shauna."

Shauna looked stunned. "For me? No, no."

"Yes, although I guess they'd be more for the good doctor here."

"Thank you, ladies," Dominik said as Shauna snatched the package from him. "That was very thoughtful, wasn't it, Shauna?"

"Dr. Coles."

Dominik turned. The nurse from the clinic had called out to him. "Ah, ladies, I have to go back to work." He leaned down and kissed each woman on the cheek. "It was an absolute pleasure meeting you today. And, Shauna, I guess you're gonna have to give me a rain check on the long story. It was good seeing you."

She nodded. "Yeah, you, too," she said.

"Call me," he said pointedly as he walked away backward.

"I'll see you Monday at the hospital."

"Or sooner," he said just before going into the clinic.

"Bye," Shauna said as she closed the trunk and opened the back door. The sisters got in and buckled up. Shauna glanced at the clinic's storefront Dominik had long since gone inside. She walked around to the driver's side as Pearl opened the front passenger door.

"He is gorgeous and it is a waste," Pearl said smiling and got in.

"Pearl," Shauna warned.

"Dr. Coles," the sisters said in unison with a smile on their faces that could only be described as radiant. "What a handsome man, and a doctor, too. Impressive," Mae added.

"Very impressive," Wanda added.

Shauna nodded. "He's just a colleague."

"Still, interesting coincidence seeing him, don't you think?"

"Too interesting if you ask me," Shauna said. "Did you know he volunteered here on weekends?"

"Me? No, of course not," Pearl said, then crossed her heart. "I swear I had no idea he came here to volunteer."

"Strange," Shauna said.

"More like serendipity," Wanda said.

"Oh, yes, most definitely serendipity," Mae acknowledged.

Wanda nodded. "I agree, although perhaps you won't be needing the rest of the items we got for you after all."

"They'll work just as well for two," Mae assured her.

Shauna drove back to Key West as Pearl and the sisters talked about the different things they found in the store. Shauna didn't pay much attention. The only thing she focused on was the road and Dominik's overly pleased expression at seeing her. She also thought about his request that she call him. No matter how tempted she was, there was no way she was going to call him. She shook her head. No, no way.

Chapter 10

Thankfully the rest of Saturday and Sunday sped by quickly. Not surprisingly she thought about Dominik the whole time. He'd planted the "call me" idea in her head and naturally all she wanted to do all weekend long was call him. Fortunately, she resisted temptation. Of course, having the gift bag filled with adult sex toys from the sisters sitting on her dresser didn't help her itchy mood.

And the itch was getting stronger, and she knew Dominik was the cause and the cure. She wanted him. She'd wanted him for a long time.

First thing Monday morning, Shauna headed to the hospital to start the E.R.'s review process. She was anxious and excited to see Dominik. She walked into the hospital and up to the main information desk. The older woman seated there looked up from her computer and smiled pleasantly. "Good morning, may I help you with something?"

"Good morning," Shauna said. "Yes, would you please tell Dr. Dominik Coles in the E.R. that Shauna Banks has arrived?"

"Yes, of course. Is Dr. Coles expecting you?"

"Yes, he is."

She nodded. "I'll call his assistant, Nora Rembrandt, to take you back to his office."

"Thank you."

A few minutes later a stern middle-aged woman with a pinched face and half glasses hanging around her neck turned a corner and came walking down the hall. She looked around, then spotted Shauna standing near the desk. "Good morning, are you here for Dr. Coles?"

"Yes, I am."

"He's in a meeting right now. He asked me to take you to the conference room and to make sure you had everything you needed. I'll be happy to answer any questions you might have to get you started."

"Actually, I do need to know where to find Lost and Found. I believe I lost a flash drive in the E.R. the last time I was here. I was told by security that I could check this morning."

"Okay. I can check for you and see if a flash drive has been turned in." She glanced at her watch. "The hospital services department is located near the cafeteria and opens in an hour."

Mine at Last

"Thank you, I'd appreciate that."

"No problem. Please come with me. I'll take you to the conference room." They walked back down the same hall, then turned to a security door. She swiped her ID badge on the wall card reader and the doors opened instantly. They walked through and she led Shauna past the main E.R. area to a side corridor.

It was still early and the hospital was quiet. The white-washed walls, the polished linoleum floor and the bright lights were all standard hospital fare. Shauna followed Nora down the empty hall. Neither spoke. They passed several closed doors and offices, one with Dominik's name on the door, and kept going. Farther down the hall, Nora stopped, unlocked and opened a door. "This is it," she said, walking inside. Shauna followed.

The room was a standard-size conference room with a long table surrounded by chairs taking up most of the space. The table was stacked with seven boxes and a number of loose files. Shauna walked over and placed her briefcase on a chair and continued to look around. There were no windows and the only other furniture was a side table with a bottle of water on top.

"I wasn't sure what you needed. I hope it's okay. I got you a bottle of water," Nora said.

"Oh, yes, it's fine. Perfect, thank you."

"Is there anything else you need?"

Of course, Dominik's name popped into her head. "No, I'm good, thank you."

"Okay, I'll check Lost and Found for your flash drive

as soon as the department opens. The bathrooms are down the hall. Here's the key to the conference room door. Dr. Gilman would like the door kept locked when you're not in here. With the files…"

Shauna nodded. "Yes, of course, I understand."

"There's a phone on the side. If you need anything else, just call the operator and ask for me."

"Thank you, Nora, I'm sure I'll be fine," she said, then walked over and opened one of the boxes on the table. She pulled out the top file and read the cover. She continued with the rest of the boxes—checking to see exactly what she had to work with. As promised, this was everything she needed. She sat down, opened her laptop and began working. Nora came back to the door an hour and a half later.

"Ms. Banks, I just checked with Lost and Found. No flash drives have been dropped off in the last three weeks. If someone did pick it up, they didn't turn it in, at least not yet. I'll check again later on today."

Shauna nodded. "Okay. Thanks for checking."

"No problem." She walked out and closed the door behind her.

Hours later Shauna looked at her watch. It was much later than she thought, well past one o'clock. Just as she opened another file, there was a light knock on the closed door. "Come in," she said.

The door opened and Dominik looked in, smiling. "Hi."

"Hi," she said.

"May I come in?" he asked.

"Sure."

He walked in carrying two bottles of water. "I would ask you how it's going, but that might be against the rules."

"There are no rules."

"Interesting. That's good to know. So, how's it going?"

"Fine, it's going fine," she said only half smiling. "There's a lot of information to go through, but I have what I need."

"Good. I thought you could use a break and also I thought you might be thirsty," he said, placing the bottles on the table in front of her.

"Actually, I am thirsty. Thank you," she said, having finished the other water bottle Nora left her. "That was kind of you."

"You say that like it's a surprise."

She sighed and closed the file she'd been reading. "Not exactly a surprise, but let's face it, you and I get along like oil and water. We're not exactly pals."

"Sure we are. And after Saturday, I would have guessed we're…"

"Hold up. I need to stop you before this gets any more complicated than it already is. What happened last weekend was…"

He smiled. "How are the sisters?" he interrupted.

"They're fine. Very brazen and very brash," she said.

"Yes, they are that," he said, chuckling. "I like them."

"You'll be happy to know they liked you, too."

"About their suggestion, you and I together. I was thinking…"

"I hope you didn't take them seriously."

"As a matter of fact, I did. I've been thinking about it," he said, coming around to her side of the table.

Me, too, nonstop, she answered mentally. "Oh," she said, then swallowed hard.

"Yes." He smiled. Pearly-white teeth made her heart stammer. "I like the idea of you and me together."

Yes, I do, too. "I think we need to keep this professional."

"No, you don't," he said, moving closer to her.

No, I don't.

"You're just as curious as I am, aren't you?"

Yes! "What makes you think that?"

He smiled. "Women don't usually passionately kiss complete strangers they're not attracted to. There's obviously sexual chemistry between us. So, the question is what are we going to do about it?" He leaned back against the table's edge looking down at her.

Have wild, buck naked sex right here, right now. "Nothing. Ignore it. We're two rational adults. We can do that."

His smile widened. "I have a better idea." He leaned over and pulled her to her feet. His lips were just inches from hers. Her heart thundered. She wanted this and she knew he knew it. Her lips parted just enough. His lips touched hers gently, then again and again, each time holding on slightly longer and longer. Kiss after kiss they leaned in just enough for their mouths to meet. Then the intensity began and the passion increased.

He leaned in, just barely brushing the tips of her nipples. She moaned, savoring the sweetness of his mouth. A flood of desire swept through her body, burning her insides from top to bottom. He had lit her flame and her body was on fire. Her heart began to pound, meeting and matching the momentum of his. She was falling and losing control. She knew this wasn't the place or the time for this. She slowly pulled away, easing back. They were both breathless and drunk with desire when the kiss ended.

"Hmm, that was nice," he muttered. "I think we should do that more often."

Yes, me, too. She looked into his dark, smoldering eyes. "I bet you do, but for the sake of our current working relationship, we should maybe not."

"Are you sure that's what you want to do?" he asked. She didn't respond, but her answer was in her eyes. "I am attracted to you, Shauna, and you're attracted to me. Let's just take it from there."

Yes, absolutely. But she didn't respond for a while. She closed her eyes and took a step back. "Dominik, I will concede I'm attracted to you. You already know that. But some attractions are impossible. This one is impossible."

"Why?"

"Because."

He smiled. "Not an answer."

"Our positions here need to be considered. We can't just jump into bed and then act like nothing happened between us. This will get emotional and complicated."

"What if this was…"

"…just physical?" she asked.

"Yes. No strings, commitments or expectations. No emotions."

She half smiled as she considered the idea of just once fulfilling her fantasy of being with Dominik. The idea was almost too tempting to resist. She bit at her lower lip, then shook her head. "Emotions always get involved."

"Ah, but that's where you're wrong, my sweet." He was just about to say more when his cell phone beeped. "Excuse me." He answered as Shauna stepped back and grabbed a bottle of water, opened it and took a long swig. She didn't realize her mouth was bone-dry. "I have to get back to the E.R.," he said. She nodded.

"I look forward to finishing this conversation soon." He walked out.

Shauna released the breath she'd been holding. She took another long sip of water. There was no way she was going to finish that conversation with him. If she busied herself, there was no way she'd have time to talk. So, she threw herself into the job.

For the next few hours she kept one eye on the door just in case Dominik came back. But he didn't. Then she began to wonder what happened to him and if he'd changed his mind about everything. She found herself more disappointed than she expected to be. She spent the rest of the afternoon buried in her work. At three-thirty she decided to find a cafeteria and get something to eat. She locked the conference room and headed out, making sure to stay as far away from the E.R. as possible.

Following the signs, she found her way to the cafeteria on the lower level. She passed the hospital services department on the way and decided to stop and ask about her flash drive. Just as Nora said earlier, it had not been found. She continued to the cafeteria. With lunch long over and dinner not yet started, the place was completely empty, except for a few cafeteria workers laughing and talking at a table in the corner. She grabbed a chicken-salad sandwich, chips and an iced tea, then headed back up to the conference room.

She ate and worked, getting a lot more done than she expected. It wasn't until her cell phone rang that she stopped for a minute. "Hi, Pearl. How are you?"

"I'm doing well. How are you?"

"Good. I started working on the hospital review today. As a matter of fact I'm here now."

"How's it going?"

"Pretty much as I anticipated," she said.

"I hope that's a good thing."

"It is, for now at least. So, what are you up to this evening? Can I take you out to dinner tonight?"

"Oh, I can't. Actually, I'm headed out of town for a few days. A friend of mine just called. She isn't doing well, so I'm gonna drive up and visit for a few days. That's why I called. Would you do me a huge favor and stop by the house a couple times this week to make sure everything is okay?"

"Of course. Sure, I'll definitely stop by. Is there anything else you need or anything I can do?"

"No, just stop by. Mind you, if you'd like to stay over, you're perfectly welcome. Your old bedroom is still there."

"No, I'm fine at the hotel. I have everything already set up."

"Okay. I'll leave a key in the usual spot and the alarm-system code is the same. I'll be back in a few days."

"Okay. Have a safe trip and I hope your friend feels better soon."

"Thank you so much. I'll see you at the end of the week."

"Pearl, one more thing. About Dominik and…"

"Go for it. You're both adults, single and God knows you're seriously attracted to each other—believe me, the man is more than interested. He never took his eyes off you the other day. And I know you've had an itch for him for years. Need I say more? Enjoy."

"Thanks, Pearl."

"Anytime. All right, I'll see you soon."

"Okay. See ya," Shauna said, then disconnected.

She smiled slyly as she thought about the real possibility of being with Dominik. There was nothing holding her back. She looked at the time. It was already well after six. She decided to call it a day. She put the files away and grabbed a pad of questions for Dominik she'd been accumulating all day. She gathered her things, turned off the light and locked the door.

She knocked on Dominik's door and waited. He didn't answer. She knocked again. There was still no answer.

"He's in the E.R. right now. There was a pretty bad accident with a few major incidents earlier. Did you need me to get him?"

Shauna turned and saw a nurse walking down the hall toward her. "Oh, no, that's okay. I'm sure he's busy."

"Do you want to leave your name?"

"That's okay. I'll catch up with him later."

"I'm Donna Pullman. I'm the chief nursing officer.

"Nice to meet you. I'm Shauna Banks."

"I heard you're from the Cura Medical Group," she added.

Shauna had asked Dr. Gilman that her presence in the hospital be kept as quiet as possible. The last thing she needed was a hundred questions from concerned employees. But she knew word would get out. It always did. "Yes, I am."

"Is the buyout going through?" she asked.

"I don't know. I haven't heard anything one way or the other."

"I hope not. I like this hospital exactly like it is."

"Compared to other hospitals, it's pretty outdated, isn't it?"

"Yeah, but that's part of its charm and character."

Shauna wanted to tell her that charm and character had nothing to do with medical care and service.

At some point, everything needed to be updated. "I guess we'll see. Have a good evening," she said and then started down the hall to the exit.

"I'll tell Dr. Coles you were looking for him."

Shauna nodded. She'd rather she didn't, but explaining that would be senseless. "Thank you."

Shauna followed the signs back to the E.R. exit. As she passed the waiting room, she glanced over and saw it practically full. She knew Dominik was busy. She continued to the door.

"Hey, you're leaving already?"

She turned and saw Dominik walking up behind her. "Hi. Yeah, I'm leaving," she said, waiting for him to catch up.

"I was told you were looking for me."

"I stopped by your office. I had a few questions for you."

"Do you want to ask me now?"

She glanced behind him briefly. "I can see you're busy. They can wait."

"Actually, I'm taking a break right now. Come on back."

She nodded and followed him back to his office. He opened the door and she walked inside. As soon as he closed the door, he pulled her into his arms and kissed her. She wrapped her arms around his neck and kissed him back. They reveled in the embrace until the need for air parted them. He held her tight in his arms and she held on to him. After a while she leaned back and looked up into his eyes. "You look exhausted."

"It's been a long day."

She nodded. "I heard there was a bad accident."

"Yeah, a three-car accident, one with six passengers inside," he said. "The cleanup is pretty messy."

"I'm sorry."

"So, you have questions for me," he said. "Shoot."

She pulled her notepad from her briefcase and asked her questions. He answered, giving her as much information as possible. For the next twenty minutes he explained method and principles related to E.R. procedure. When they were done, she had a very good understanding of how the E.R. ran previously to his management and the mistakes made under Dr. Bowman's tenure. "Okay, that's it for now."

"Good. Now I have a question."

"Shoot."

"Have you thought about our previous conversation?"

"I have."

"And?"

"And," she said, then paused and shook her head, "I don't know what to say. My job requires me to be extremely discreet."

"As does mine."

"Yes, of course. What I mean is that I don't jump in and out of bed easily. And in most cases I don't spend enough time in one location to form any romantic or sexual attachments, so this is very different for me."

He nodded. "I understand."

"Why me?" she asked curiously. "I have a feeling the women around here just about worship you. As a matter of fact, I've heard they actually adore you."

He chuckled. "I don't know about all that. But I do know that I like being with you, talking with you. You say oil and water—I say stimulating foreplay. And then there's something in your eyes that takes my breath away."

She took a deep breath and swallowed hard. She suddenly felt hot. "Surrender is difficult for me. I need to think about this."

He smiled. "Take all the time you need."

She smiled, too. "Good answer."

Before he responded again, there was a knock on his door. Dr. Gilman stuck her head in. Her eyes widened at finding Shauna sitting there. She smiled tightly. There was an awkwardness as she came in. "Ms. Banks, hi," Dr. Gilman said, looking from Shauna to Dominik. "I hope everything is okay and I'm not interrupting?"

"Everything's fine, and no, you're not interrupting. Come in. Join us," Dominik said.

"Ms. Banks, I thought you'd have gone home by now."

Shauna looked at her watch and frowned. "Is that the time? Actually, you're right, it's late and I still have some work to do." She put her notepad in her briefcase and stood.

"Well, I hope Dr. Coles has taken very good care of you."

"Yes. I had some questions about E.R. procedure and he was kind enough to stay and answer them for me. I definitely have a better understanding of how the E.R. runs," she said.

"Good. Are there any questions I can answer for you?"

"I'll more than likely have questions for you in a few days."

"Fine. Just let me know and I'll be available."

"I will. Good night, Doctors." She nodded to Dominik and then walked out.

"Please tell me that wasn't another altercation," she said.

"What do you mean, 'altercation'?"

"I heard about Friday night," she said, shaking her head. "Your very heated discussion in the E.R. foyer with Shauna is all over the hospital. I asked you to help her, not alienate her. We need this, Dominik. We need her to give us a favorable review. There's no way this hospital is going to survive without the Cura Medical Group's backing. Whatever happened, whatever I just walked in on, you need to fix it now."

"Margaret, relax, it wasn't an altercation."

She looked at him hard. "Okay, good. I need you to be on point and work closely with her. I need to know if she's leaning toward going through with the buyout or not."

"How am I supposed to do that?"

"Be creative. Carry on," she said, then walked out.

Dominik gathered his things to leave for the day. He walked out the long way, passing the conference room just in case Shauna had gone back there. The door was closed and locked and the lights were off. He continued to the exit, waving to his E.R. staff and then to Rodney at the security desk before heading out for the night. He got halfway to his car.

"Dr. Dom, Dr. Dom."

Dominik turned and saw Lindy, a longtime patient, running through the parking lot to catch up with him. "Hi, Lindy. Are you okay?"

"Hi, Doc. I'm doing fine." She smiled happily, out of breath.

"Are you taking your medication like you're supposed to?"

"Yes," she said.

"Good. Then I'll see you later," he said and turned to continue walking to the doctor's parking area.

"But wait, I just wanted to give you something. I found it last week in the E.R. waiting room. It was on the floor where I was sitting before." She held up a small flash drive. "I think it belongs to one of those reporters. I tried to look at what was on it just in case it was important, but it's all scrambled up. I think it's broken. Anyway, I didn't want to throw it away just in case it might still be something useful. Is it the hospital's?"

Dominik looked at the small black drive knowing it didn't belong to the hospital. But the possibility that someone had accidently left it in the waiting room was very real. "No, it doesn't belong to the hospital, but I'm sure it belongs to someone. And I'm sure they've been looking for it. You need to turn it in to security and they'll take care of it."

"Okay," she said happily. "Are you going back inside?"

"No, I'm going home now. I'll see you later."

"Okay. I'll give this to Rodney. Have a good night, Doc," she said and then hurried inside.

Dominik went to his car. As soon as he got in, his cell phone beeped. There was an email message from the hospital. He opened and read it. It was Rodney notifying him about Lindy's found flash drive. Dominik frowned. He had no idea why Rodney would send him a message about something intended for Lost and Found. He got out and went back into the E.R.

"Hi, Doc. I thought you might want to take care of this personally," Rodney said. "This is the flash drive the lady from the Cura Group was looking for over the weekend. I could put it in Lost and Found, but I know she's anxious to find it." Rodney gave him the drive.

"Thanks, Rodney. I'll take care of it."

Rodney nodded. "Have a good night, Doc."

On the drive home, Dominik considered going by the Gateway Inn to drop off the flash drive, but he knew going over there this late at night might be construed as something else. He decided to wait and give it to her the following day.

By the time he got home, he felt recharged. A surge

of energy pumped through him. He showered, slipped on sweatpants and stepped out onto his balcony, looking out over the view he'd paid an astronomical price for but seldom enjoyed. It was the splendor of Key West with a breathtaking coastal view of the ocean and a stunning sunset.

He went back inside, grabbed his briefcase and set it on the desk in his home office. He pulled out his laptop and the flash drive Rodney had given him. He turned on his laptop and looked up Shauna's company on the internet. There was no website, but there was a Maryland mailing address and email.

He picked up the flash drive and looked at it, wondering what it contained. Popping it into his computer would be so easy, but he knew he wouldn't do that. Still, a slow, easy smile crossed his lips. He typed in the email address he'd found on the internet and sent a note to Shauna asking if she was missing a flash drive. He waited. There was no reply.

Convincing himself that he wasn't disappointed wasn't as easy as he'd hoped. He had wanted to see Shauna. He looked at the laptop's small screen. All of a sudden, work didn't seem like such a good idea. He saved the file, then closed the program. Just as he began to close the laptop, the email message light began blinking. He checked his mail. The smile on his face broadened.

Chapter 11

Shauna stayed up late most nights. Tonight was no exception. The hotel room was dark except for a single lamp on the nightstand brightly illuminating the area beside the bed. She sat cross-legged with her laptop balanced on her knees. She had the TV on, but she wasn't watching it. For the past half hour, she had been going through the notes she'd taken earlier that day. Not surprisingly, it wasn't her best work. Her initial assessments weren't as reasoned and focused as they usually were, which meant she needed to redo most of them. It was obvious to her that she had been distracted.

She could tell exactly when it happened. The second spotted Dominik Coles standing in the conference room doorway looking at her, everything went sideways. Her heart thumped. Just the memory of looking up and seeing him there made her nerves shudder. She moved the laptop to the side, then looked around the cookie-cutter room, finally focusing on the television screen.

A commercial had just come on showing singles talking about searching for love. They were smiling and happily describing their lives after joining the advertised singles-matching program. Shauna rolled her eyes to the ceiling and chuckled. A phone number and dozens of supposedly single men on the other end was a fairy-tale empty promise preying on the perpetually hopeful. She shook her head, discounting the ridiculous claims of finding love so easily. "Finding love is not as easy as a phone call," she said to the television.

Lately, she had begun to wonder if she would ever find love herself. Where was her Prince Charming or her knight in shining armor? When the answer didn't readily come, she got up and walked over to the large plate-glass window and pulled the drapes aside. The hotel wasn't the best in the city, but that never mattered a lot to her. She never paid much attention. As long as the room was clean and had the essentials, she was fine. But this evening she would have loved to step out onto a balcony to get some fresh air. Instead she just looked out over the skyline peppered with the city's night lights.

Bathed in complete darkness, the night's sparkling lights shone and sparkled against the many streets and buildings. Her view was of the downtown area, but as a resort city, there wasn't much of a business district.

From the tenth floor she saw streets blocked out, building roofs and treetops, and of course far in the distance she knew there was the ocean's horizon. Even though it was late, the streets were lively with tourists and pedestrians still shopping and walking around.

A quiet sadness washed over her as she thought about her last evening with Pearl. It was great seeing her but also sad and distressing. Not because seeing her reminded her of everything she'd lost—it was what Pearl had said about her life now. She had a beautiful home in a secluded neighborhood, a new car, an easy life, and still she was alone.

The sadness seemed to permeate her heart. This wasn't what she was supposed to be feeling. She closed the drapes and turned her back on the outside, then went back over to the bed and sat down.

She grabbed her laptop putting it back onto her lap. She opened the program and started reviewing what she had written earlier. Now focusing on her job, she began retyping the notes, taking a more aggressive stance on what she found in the files so far. She listed a number of questions about the waiting process and E.R. regulations that needed answering. A short while later she was completely engrossed in her job. Cross-checking and reviewing the electronic files Key West Medical had given the Cura Group for review, she was midway through reading a report from the previous team of auditors when she received an email. At first she ignored it, but then she brought up the screen. It was from Dominik. She opened and read the message.

It was simple and to the point. Are you missing a flash drive? She smiled. She replied to his email giving him her phone number and asking him to please call. A few minutes later her cell phone rang. She slowly reached over and answered. "Hello."

"Hello," Dominik said.

Her insides instantly warmed just from hearing his voice. "Hi."

"I hope I'm not calling you too late," he said.

"No, not at all. I usually stay up late working, so I was still up. I don't usually require much sleep."

"Nor do I," he said. "I see we have that in common, as well."

"Yeah, I guess we do."

"As I mentioned in the email, I have a flash drive."

"Yes, it is mine. I'd been looking for it all day. It must have fallen out of my briefcase last Friday. Where did you find it?"

"I didn't. Lindy found it and asked me about it. She told me she found it in the E.R. waiting room last week. I didn't know you'd lost it, so I told her to give it to Rodney, the security guard. He presumed it was yours. He gave it to me thinking I'd know how to contact you tonight."

"I wonder what made him think that," she said sarcastically.

"Yes, I wonder," he said.

"Still, I'll make sure to thank Rodney. When can I get it from you?"

"Whenever you like. I'll be in meetings out of the building in the morning. How about tomorrow afternoon?" he offered.

"Actually, sooner would be better. The drive has a specialized filtering program that would help with what I will be working on in the morning. It'll help me sort through data quickly and thoroughly. It makes my job a lot easier and it's one of a kind. It also has information from a previous job, so I need it back as soon as possible," she said.

"Sure. Shall I come to you now?" he said without hesitation.

Shauna looked around her hotel room and immediately spotted the toys the sisters had bought for her still in the packages on the dresser. There was no way she wanted him there. "No, I'll come to you," she said.

"Fine. I'll email my address and directions."

"Okay, thank you. I'll see you soon," Shauna said. Then, as soon as she pressed the end-call button, she stopped and thought about what she'd just done. She'd just agreed to go to Dominik's house. She picked up her cell phone to call him back and suggest they meet at a more public place, but just saying the words in her head sounded silly. What was she afraid was going to happen—a booty call? She would just go to his house, get her flash drive and come back to the hotel. No big deal.

She smiled and chuckled to herself as the stray thought of going to Dominik's house for a booty call hit her. Still, the thought was certainly interesting. She could just imagine what it would be like. He had a body that was made for fun even back in high school. She could only imagine what his body looked like now— thick, ripped muscles, tight, defined abs and a rear firm enough to play with all night long. She shook her head, quickly shrugging off the craziness of her wayward sex thoughts.

She re-dressed in her jeans and a button-down shirt, grabbed her purse and keys, and headed out. She checked her cell phone for the address and directions. She knew exactly where he lived. It wasn't too far from Pearl's house, from her old neighborhood.

She pulled up in front of his house. She glanced over, seeing the lights on and the front door open. She got out, and as soon as she locked the car door, the heavens opened and rain poured down in a torrential flood.

With no umbrella and no hat, she made a mad dash to the front door. She rang the bell. Dominik came a few seconds later. But she was completely soaked by then. He held the door open and she hurried inside. The air-conditioning chilled her instantly. She shivered and wiped the rain from her cheeks and forehead. "Hi," she said.

"Come on in. You're soaked. When did it start raining?" he asked.

"Um, just now. I pulled up, got out and there was a

cloud burst. I couldn't believe it. Great timing, right?" she said breathlessly from the short run down his front path.

"Come on into the living room. I'll get you a towel."

"No, no, that's okay. I'm gonna get soaked again as soon as I leave. I'll just grab the flash drive and get out of your way."

"You know you could stay and wait until the rain slacks up. I'm sure it's just a passing shower. It'll be over in a few minutes."

Just then, lightning flashed. Shauna jumped closer to Dominik and held her breath. Instinctively he placed his hand at the base of her back. "Are you okay?"

She nodded. "Oh, yeah. I didn't expect lightning. I'm not a big fan of thunderstorms." A rumble of thunder in the distance made them both look up. "Well, it's late and I don't want to disturb your evening any more than I have," she said, looking around curiously.

Dominik watched her. "There's no one here but us," he said softly.

She'd been caught and felt silly. "Oh, I just hope I wasn't intruding."

"Not at all. I'll get the flash drive for you."

He walked away and disappeared into a room across the hall. Shauna presumed it was his office. There was another bright flash of lightning and soon after a loud clap of thunder seemed to rock the house. The lights blinked. Shauna closed her eyes and tried to still her panic. She felt the sickening swell of nervousness coming. Her heart raced. She took several slow, deep breaths to prevent herself from hyperventilating.

"Here's it is," Dominik said as he returned to her. The lights blinked again. He looked up. "It looks like we might lose power." Then he looked at her. "You know, you really don't need to leave right now. You're perfectly welcome to stay," he said.

Shauna nodded nervously. "No, that's okay. I'm fine, thank you." She took the drive and quickly headed to the front door.

"Shauna, wait. At least take an umbrella," Dominik said, opening the nearby closet door. He grabbed an umbrella, but Shauna had already stepped out into the pouring rain. "Shauna," he called.

She ran to the car, but the panic attack was already with her. She was breathing too hard and her body trembled uncontrollably. Her hands shook as she tried to open the door. Her keys fell. She bent down to get them, fishing through a shallow puddle. Lightning flashed and instantly a massive clap of thunder erupted right over her head. She couldn't breathe. She couldn't move.

Dominik stepped outside with the umbrella, but Shauna was already halfway down the brick path. He saw her get to her car, then run around to the driver's side. She bent down and then nothing. She never stood up. He dropped the umbrella and ran around the car and found her crumbled beside the door, shaking. He bent down and grabbed her, thinking she had fallen.

"Shauna," he called out. There was another flash of lightning and soon after, thunder.

"Shauna," he called out again. She didn't look up. He saw that her eyes were closed. He scooped her up into his arms and carried her back down the brick path to the front door. He opened it and hurried inside. Heading right to his office, he sat Shauna down on the thick cushioned sofa. She was shivering. He grabbed the remote control and turned on the fireplace. Then he ran and grabbed towels from the adjacent bathroom. He came back into the room and saw that Shauna was exactly as he'd left her.

She was trembling and staring straight ahead. Lightning flashed and he hurried to her side before thunder rumbled soon after. He sat close and wrapped his arms around her body, holding her tight. When the next rumble came, he gripped her even tighter. She huddled close and he stroked her back, covering her with the dry towel. "It's okay. I'm here," he whispered soothingly. He kissed her forehead and she held on tighter. She closed her eyes and let the moment last as long as she could.

After a while the storm passed and only a few low rumbles of thunder reverberated in the distance. He could feel her body calm down and relax beside him. He still held her close. She took a deep breath. "I'm wet," she said.

"Yes, you are. Do you want to take your clothes off?"

"Um…"

"I promise to be a perfect gentleman."

"That's no fun," she said.

He chuckled. "Can I get you something to drink?" he offered.

"Water," she said.

He got up and came back with two bottles of water. He untwisted the caps on both and handed her one. She took a few sips. "Better?" he asked. She nodded. "Panic attack," he said.

She nodded. "Yes, I have them once in a while, but not for a long time. Thunder and lightning storms are my trigger. A doctor suggested I take anxiety medication, but I'm not a big fan of taking pills. Therapy is just talk, and it's not like I can't avoid them. I usually lie down, put on earphones and listen to music. It passes. But getting caught like tonight…"

"No earphones."

She nodded and leaned away from him. "Exactly. Thank you."

"For what?" he asked.

She turned to him. "For being here for me."

"My pleasure," he said, smiling.

A moment of silence passed between them. "It sounds like the storm's passed. I'd better go."

"Actually, as a medical professional, specifically as a doctor, I can't advise you leave right now."

"I'm fine. I promise."

"Sorry," he said, shaking his head, "I took the Hippocratic oath and that trumps your 'I'm fine' promise.

Besides, I could use a little snack. How about you?" Just as he said it, there was another rumble of thunder.

"Sure, but I have to confess, I can't help you much. I'm not the greatest cook in the world," Shauna admitted.

"That's okay. My sister is. We hung out last weekend and she sent me home with a couple plates of food." He stood up and reached his hand down to her. She grasped it and stood. They both instantly remembered the last time he'd done this. He smiled. She smiled. "This way."

He led her from the office to the kitchen. The lights were already on and a wonderful aroma wafted from the oven. "I had just put a couple of plates in when you rang the doorbell."

"Knowing that I'd stay, of course," she said.

"Let's just say I hoped you might." He walked over to the oven, grabbed two mitts and opened the door. Shauna followed, watching him.

"You actually look like you know what you're doing."

"I'm not too bad in the kitchen, but my sister is the professional in the family. She's an incredible chef. She owns a café in town."

"Which sister?" she asked.

"Nikita. The café is called Nikita's Café."

Shauna smiled. "Really? I was just there Friday. A friend wanted me to pick up dessert for our dinner."

"A friend," he repeated, looking alarmed.

She nodded. "Yes, a friend of my mother's, now my friend."

He pulled two plates from the oven and placed them

on the counter. His smiled broadened. "Which sister?" he repeated. She nodded. "That statement would imply that you know my family or at the very least that I have more than one sister."

She smiled, realizing she'd slipped again. "Okay, you got me."

"We do know each other, don't we?"

"No, we've never actually met, and before you ask, I don't know your sisters, your older brother or anyone else in your family. We did, however, go to the same high school a million years ago."

He nodded. "I see."

"It was a long time ago, but I remember you very well."

"Do you?" he said. She nodded. He placed a knife, fork and napkin next to the plate of food. "What year did you graduate?"

She looked down at the plate in front of her. "Wow, this looks incredible and it smells wonderful."

"Good," he said, placing another bottle of water in front of her. "Let's eat."

They ate and talked about their travels and being single. They found they had a lot more in common than they thought. Afterward he cleaned up while she helped. "You know, you're gonna make some woman a wonderful housewife someday."

He chuckled. "You think so?"

"Oh, definitely. You cook. You clean. Who could ask for anything more?" she said as she stood up and walked to the kitchen window. She looked out into the backyard. It was dark and impossible to tell if it was still raining or not.

"This way," Dominik said. He opened the back door for her. They stepped out onto the veranda. The storm had cooled the air and there was a nice breeze. He toggled a light switch and instantly the yard was softly illuminated. A fine mist wafted from the heated pool and the surrounding grounds.

"Wow, this is really nice," she said, looking around. There was a large pool and sauna with a waterfall. Directly across were a fountain and a beautiful flower-and-shrub garden inlay with various-size rocks and small boulders. Then there was subdued lighting hidden in the trees and shrubs, giving the whole area a soft, dreamlike glow. Everything about it looked calm and relaxing. "I bet the view is beautiful at sunset."

"It's phenomenal. You should come back and see it. But the view from upstairs is without a doubt the most spectacular sight in the Keys," he said, standing right behind her. "Dawn is pretty nice, too."

"It stopped raining," she said. "I guess I'd better get back to the hotel. Thank you for my flash drive and everything." She turned and walked past him.

"Wait," he said, then paused. He took her hand and held it. She stopped. "What are we doing here?"

She knew what he meant, but she didn't know how to answer him. She lowered her head. "We're avoiding the obvious."

He nodded. "Yes, we are. I'll yield—I want you."

"I want you, too, but that doesn't mean we should... When I kissed you, I started something that never should have happened. And now I think we need to..."

"No," he said firmly, "this was before we kissed in the office. When I first saw you early Friday morning and then again later in the E.R., there was something. I felt it as soon as I saw you and so did you."

Shauna's heart jumped and her stomach tumbled. "Dominik."

"We're both single, consenting adults. Other than that I don't care about the dynamics of whether this is right or wrong."

"And what about our jobs?" she asked.

"You do your job and I'll do mine. We can take the emotion out and enjoy this for what it is—a physical attraction. Can you do that?"

"Dominik, I..."

The kiss came in an instant and the blinding heat from it swept her off her feet. It was quick and it was fierce. Pent-up desire had been released. Their mouths connected and sealed. His tongue delved deep into her and she met his passion with equal fervor. The scant space between their bodies vanished. He stepped forward, pressing her back against the arbor's wooden brace. She felt the hardness of his penis grind against her and her insides gelled. A low, primal groan rumbled from his throat as his hand reached between them and unbuttoned her shirt. The last two buttons were impatiently ripped off.

His nimble fingers flicked the front-snap bra and it gave way immediately. Her breasts, unrestricted, bounced free. His large, strong hands grabbed each and his thumbs toyed with her nipples. A second later he tore his mouth from her swollen lips and eased down her neck to her breasts. She gasped, feeling the air around her quickly evaporate. Her body jerked and trembled as she anticipated his next move.

His hot mouth enveloped her breast, one and then the other. His torturous tongue flicked and licked her hardened nipples. Quivers and shivers surged through her body as wave after wave of rapture overtook her. Her legs weakened. There was no way she could focus on anything except what Dominik was doing to her body right now.

His hand slid down to her stomach and then between her legs. She gasped. Her jeans were wet. He stroked her gently. Her head rolled back. She looked up at the trellis of scented flowers above. He kissed her neck and earlobe with loving madness as he unsnapped her jeans and tore down the zipper. Her jeans eased down her legs. Her mouth went dry as she began to pant.

She closed her eyes, feeling his hand on her skin pulling at her elastic waistband. Her body trembled, arching as she thrusted her gyrating hips back and forth, wanting more. He gave her exactly what she needed. With one finger stroking the nub of her pleasure outside and two teasing her G-spot inside, she felt as if her body was being torn apart from the inside out. It was sweet, tormented rapture. She wiggled and squirmed against his masterful play and loved every minute of it.

Then she felt the surge of pleasure coming on her. "Dominik," she muttered. He flicked both swollen nubs at the same time and like a switch being turned on, her body ignited. She screamed. He did it again and again. She screamed each time louder and longer. Then the last time she gasped and held her breath.

"Breathe," he whispered.

"Can't. I can't," she stammered.

He stopped and gripped her in his arms tightly. She took a fast breath and exhaled slowly. The next breath came easier. She slumped against him. Her body was spent. She'd never experienced anything like that before.

Dominik leaned his head down and kissed her neck tenderly. His hot breath scorched her skin. "Shauna, look at me," he said as he leaned back and tipped her chin upward. She looked up into his eyes. His pupils were dark and dilated. "You know where this is going," he whispered.

She nodded her head. "I know," she said, swallowing hard but not moving an inch. Common sense begged her to withdraw, to leave, but want and need cemented her in place. It seemed the more she knew this was forbidden, the more she wanted it. Yes, they kissed, touched and only heaven knew what he just did to her because her body was still tingling, but crossing that final line meant no turning back. She was playing with fire.

"When you're ready, I'll be here. Go," he whispered, then stepped back and released her. She nodded and walked away, leaving him standing alone.

Chapter 12

For the next four days both Shauna and Dominik, through an unspoken accordance, put what had happened between them and their personal feelings on hold. They stayed focused on doing their respective jobs. Neither spoke about the night they were together. Shauna buried herself in her work. The review was going well and in a couple of weeks all this would be behind her. She'd made a good start separating the job into several components to present as a whole later on.

It was mostly reviewing, reading and auditing records and accounts to justify actions and procedures taken. She needed to diagram them out in financial records and balance sheets to verify the noted financial statements. It was all very technical and analytical, but the end question was simple: Did the hospital's E.R. department meet its financial responsibility and would it exceed it in the future?

Hospitals seldom made exorbitant amounts of money for their investors; it wasn't their purpose. However, they could be financially viable if prudent while taking aggressive steps and were encouraged to keep waste and mishandling to a minimum and of course maintain high production value. It was a delicate line and she'd always found the hospitals that could traverse that line.

Experience and knowledge had taught her everything she needed to know. She was good, and when facilities listened to her, they showed a very marked improvement. They could take note of her ideas, but implementation based on her fact-finding was their responsibility.

She closed another file and added it to the top of the stack. She put the lid on the box and nodded. The first two boxes were done. She took a deep breath and looked at the remaining four boxes. "Four more," she muttered to herself.

She decided to take a break and go to the cafeteria to get something to drink. She went downstairs, grabbed an iced tea and a bag of potato chips. She sat down in the empty cafeteria facing the window and watched the skyline.

She thought about Dominik's view and wondered what it looked like from his bedroom. Thinking about Dominik was a moment of weakness and she enjoyed every second of it. She'd seen him since the rainy night, of course, but he hadn't mentioned what happened and neither had she. It was as if it never even happened. She almost thought she dreamed it.

He'd understood her fears and he'd held her. No one had ever done that before. She never let anyone get that close. She closed her eyes and instantly felt the shadow of his body pressed behind her and his arms holding her tight. No man had ever touched her like that and no man had ever given her the power. But he was right, she wasn't ready for him.

He could show her a whole new world and she needed his tutelage. She may not be ready, but she was definitely willing. "Tonight," she whispered as she nodded her head and smiled. "Tonight."

"Ms. Banks?"

Shauna turned around and looked up to where Dr. Gilman was standing behind her, smiling. "Dr. Gilman, hi, good evening."

"Well, hello, I thought that was you. How are you today?"

"I'm doing well, thank you."

"I was just about to head back upstairs when I saw you sitting down here all alone. Taking a much-needed break?" she asked.

"Yes, I am."

"I've been meaning to stop down to see if you need anything."

"Actually, I have everything I need. It's going quicker than I expected."

"Good, good. So, Ms. Banks…" Margaret began.

"Please, Doctor, call me Shauna."

"I will, and please call me Margaret." Shauna nodded. "So," Margaret continued, "Shauna, how's everything going?"

"So far so good. I just finished reviewing the first two boxes of files. I'd say I'll be out of your hair in another two weeks or even sooner."

"Having you around is an absolute pleasure. I hate to say this, but the last two teams from Cura spent most of their time flirting with the doctors and nurses and trying to get free medical advice."

"Really?" Shauna said.

"Sadly, yes. Oh, they did the review, but it took months. That's why everything is so rush, rush now. And even then, they couldn't give us any indication of how the review was going."

"It's hard to give any definitive answers when there's still so much of the process left to do."

"Can you tell me something?" Margaret began as she took a seat beside Shauna.

"If I can, sure," Shauna said.

"The last two teams wrote up their reviews. Who got copies?"

"Copies went to the Cura Medical Group board of directors, the CEO, CFO, COO and to me."

"And who writes the final report?"

"I do."

"And you're their consultant."

"I'm an independent consultant. Cura is my biggest client. I have others."

"I see. So, tell me, how are you finding our little medical center?"

"The people here are very kind and generous."

"And Dr. Coles?" she asked.

Shauna looked at Margaret. Her eyes widened. The question was totally out of the blue. "What about him?"

"I just want to make sure the two of you are getting along."

"Yes, we are. We're fine."

"Because I can have someone else be your main contact."

"No, Dr. Coles is fine," she said too quickly.

"Oh, good, good. I'm pleased to hear it. So, is this your first time in Key West?"

"No, I spent a few years here years ago. As a matter of fact, I graduated from Key West High School."

Margaret's eyes instantly lit up. "Really? What a coincidence. Quite a few members of our staff also graduated from Key West High. As a matter of fact, Dr. Coles graduated from Key West."

"Really?"

"Oh, yes. Actually, I'm surprised you don't know him or his family. He has three sisters and a brother. They all have Russian names. Let's see, there's Dominik, Mikhail, Natalia, Nikita and Tatiana. You don't know them?" she asked.

"I was only at the school for a couple of years. I didn't know a lot of the students there."

"Oh, that explains it."

"Well, Margaret," Shauna said, gathering her things, "I guess I'd better get back to work now and let you get back, as well. I know running a medical center is a thankless and nearly impossible job."

"Yes, it is that," Margaret said, standing to leave. "It was good talking to you, Shauna. I'm sure we'll chat again soon. Oh, one more thing. I'll be out of the office at a conference most of next week. If you need anything, I'm sure Dr. Coles will be happy to assist you."

"I'm sure he will. Thank you."

"You're very welcome," Margaret said. She started to walk away, but then turned back around. "Shauna, please, I need you to be honest with me. You've seen the two reports and are looking through them and double-checking some of the findings. Please, tell me, will the buyout happen?"

"Margaret, I can't tell you that. I honestly don't know. I don't make the final decision."

"You made decisions for Cura Medical in the past. Did they listen to you ultimately?"

Shauna weighed whether telling Margaret the truth would jeopardize anything. "Ultimately, yes, they did listen to me."

Margaret frowned and then nodded. "Thank you. That was very helpful. I appreciate your candor. You have a good evening. Carry on."

As soon as Margaret left, Shauna got up and headed back to the conference room. She went through and sorted the next box of files in preparation for the coming week. Just as she finished, she received a text message from Pearl.

Pearl: All is well here. Everything okay with you?

Shauna: Yes, just fine. How's your friend?

Pearl: Doing a little better, still ill. I've decided to stay a few more days.

Shauna: Sounds good. I've checked the house—no problems.

Pearl: Good. I'll text you later. Have a great weekend. Get out of that stuffy hotel and have some fun. That's an order.

Shauna smiled as she read the text.

Shauna: I am. As a matter of fact, I'm going out this evening to see a little more of the city.

Pearl: Not alone, I hope.

Shauna: We'll see....

Pearl: Don't forget the sisters' gift bag for you. They're expecting you to put it to good use and I know a very attractive doctor who'd be perfect to play doctor with. I promised your mother that I'd take care of you and that's exactly what I intend to do. Even if you're gonna be stubborn about it. Call the man!

Shauna: SMH. Focus on your sick friend. I'll see you
when you get back. Be safe.
Pearl: I get the hint. See you soon.

Shauna shook her head as she read Pearl's last message. She knew her mother had asked Pearl to look out
for her and Pearl had been wonderful. But this was something she couldn't help her with. She had to do this on
her own. She continued getting the next box ready for
the following week. When she finished, she locked the
door and headed to Dominik's office.

Dominik, for the most part, concentrated on running
the E.R. and only stopped by to see Shauna once or
twice—mostly at the end of the day to see if she had any
review-related questions for him. He never mentioned
what happened between them, giving her space and let-
ting her make the next move.

Toward the end of the week, a stubborn tropical storm
had settled along the Gulf Coast, unleashing heavy rains
and thunderstorms. It ushered in the area's official start
to hurricane season. The past few days, the hospital E.R.
had been packed with vacationers and Key West residents coming in with a barrage of simple and not-so-
simple ailments ranging from cuts and laceration to broken limbs, and panic and heart attacks.

In preparation for any possible weather-related sce-
nario, Dominik met regularly with the city's emergency-
preparedness committee and focused his attention on

additional supplies and evacuation protocols. He stocked up on antibiotics, inhalers, insulin and medication for eye infections, hypertension and seizure control with additional focus on dehydration and depression—two lesser-attended weather-related ailments.

Because the medical center had already seen a stark increase in common household ailments, Dominik extended his working hours even more. It seemed by the time he left to go home, it was time for him to come back in. By Friday the weather had settled into a routine of steady rain and passing thunderstorms. Friday evening he stayed later than usual and by chance stopped by the conference room hoping Shauna might still be there. She wasn't. He went back to his office just as his cousin Stephen walked up to meet him. "Hey, what are you doing here?" he said. "Are you still on duty?"

"I had some official business to take care of here, and I thought I'd stop by and check on you when I finished."

"How are Mia and the baby?"

"She's good, getting big and looking sexier than ever, and the baby's right on schedule. So, what's going on?" Stephen asked, following him into the office.

Dominik shook his head. "It was a long day and a long week."

"Yeah, I heard about the craziness here on Monday. Pretty rough."

"It was bad, a DUI with three kids in the car—totally ridiculous. It didn't have to happen. Three fatalities. What are people thinking?"

Stephen shook his head. "I see it all the time. And that's just it—they're not thinking," Stephen said.

They both seemed to lapse into a quiet sadness, having seen way too much senseless death and thoughtless drama.

"So, Dom, what's going on with you, my man?"

"What do you mean?"

"Just what I said, what's going on with you?"

"I'm doing okay, tired, whipped, beat-down, you know the drill. Just working hard and getting the job done. Running this department is a lot more time-consuming that I thought."

"Yeah, I'm sure it is, but that's not it. Last week at the house you were totally out of it. I asked you a question twice and you heard me the third time. I've never seen you so distracted. So, do you want to tell me about her?"

Dominik shook his head and chuckled. His cousin always seemed to have a sixth sense when it came to troubled hearts. He connected with his Mia's father and wound up falling in love with his daughter before he even met her. "She's a consultant working for the Cura Medical Group. She's only here for a few weeks, so I know nothing can really happen between us, but man, there's something about her." He shook his head steadily, then took a deep breath and blew it out slowly.

Stephen chuckled. "Man, don't you know a few weeks, a few days or a few hours is sometimes all it takes to start a lifetime together? Believe me, I've learned that the hard way. Remember, Mia was here for only a few weeks, too."

"Whoa, you make this sound like a love thing."

"Isn't it?" Stephen asked.

"No," Dominik said quickly. Stephen chuckled softly. "No, no," Dominik repeated. Stephen started laughing out loud. "All right, all right, truthfully, I don't know what it is. I just know I can't get her out of my mind. I saw her last week sitting in the E.R. waiting room. I looked over and she looked up. If I didn't know it was medically impossible, I'd say my heart stopped beating, then jump-started again—no paddle, no charge, no nothing. I knew her or rather I remembered her from high school."

"She went to school with us?" Stephen asked.

Dominik nodded. "She was there in our senior year. She was quiet and totally unassuming. When all the other girls were jumping in our faces, she didn't. She stayed back. That's what got my attention then. And her eyes are gorgeous. They're cautious and guarded with a fundamental sadness, like she's carrying the weight of the world on her shoulders."

"So, this is just the doctor in you wanting to heal her?"

"No, this is the man in me wanting to love her," he said, then stopped short hearing the words that came out of his mouth.

"Yeah, you said that. You know I've never known you

to be this enamored by a woman," Stephen said, pulling out his notepad. "What's her name?"

"No way, you're not doing a workup on her."

"Of course I am. What's the sense in having a cousin who's a sheriff if you're not gonna let me use my connections to cut through the red tape? You know I do it for Mikhail all the time."

"With Mikhail, you'd have to. He lives his life on a high wire. He's got women coming out of the woodwork after him."

They laughed, then stopped when there was a knock on his door. "Come in," Dominik called out.

The door opened and Shauna peeked in. "Oh, I'm sorry. You're busy. I can come back another time."

"No, come in," Dominik said, standing and walking to the door. Stephen stood, as well. He smiled, already knowing who she was before even being introduced. "I want you to meet someone. Shauna Banks, this is my cousin Stephen Morales."

"Hello, nice to meet you," she said, extending her hand to shake.

"Shauna, it's good meeting you," Stephen said. He turned and smiled at his cousin. "All right, I gotta get home. Mia's waiting for me."

"Tell her I said hi and to take care of herself and the baby."

"I will. Shauna, it was a pleasure meeting you. Hope to see you again soon." He shook Dominik's hand, then they hugged. "Take care." Stephen left and Dominik walked back to where Shauna was standing. "I stopped by the conference room earlier. It was locked, so I thought you had already left."

She shook her head. "I must have stepped out for a minute. I'm headed out now," she said.

"Do you want to get something to eat?" he asked.

She nodded. "That sounds great, but actually, I have a better idea. I was going to stop by the Village. Would you like to join me?"

He smiled. "I'd love to. Shall I pick you up in—" he quickly glanced at his watch "—an hour and a half?"

"Sounds perfect. I'm in suite 1012."

Chapter 13

The stormy, dreary, rainy weather was finally at bay for the moment. The streets were pumped up and crowded with vacationers and party revelers all out celebrating and enjoying the momentary weather reprieve. Still, the heavy overcast skies threatened, but for the time being, even that didn't spoil anyone's good time. The streets were packed as nightclub after nightclub churned out loud, laughing, smiling, happy customers who simply left one bar's party and entered another's just down the block.

Dominik and Shauna watched the street scene as they ate a late-night dinner at a small outdoor bistro just on the outskirts of the Village. She had salmon and he had crab cakes. While lingering over a huge slice of pie and a bottle of white wine, they sat leisurely and talked about their jobs and his family and his travels.

Shauna sighed. "I haven't had this in years. I'd forgotten how good it can be," she said, taking another sampling of the tart citrus dessert.

"It is pretty good here. They're famous for key-lime pies."

"So, is this where it was invented?" she asked.

"Actually, no one knows exactly who invented it. They say it just caught on and grew from there with the recipe being passed down from generation to generation. But I do know it was invented here on the island."

"I used to think it was made with regular limes until my mother's best friend, Pearl, showed me her key-lime tree."

"Oh, yes, there are limes and there are key limes, two very different fruits. You need my sister Nikita to tell you about all that. She makes a key-lime tart that is pure heaven."

Shauna took one more bite, then shook her head. "I'm stuffed."

"Are you ready to go?" Dominik asked. He stood and held out his hand to her. She took it and smiled.

"Thank you. This was nice."

"I hope you're not ready to go in yet. The night's just begun."

"What do you have in mind?"

He wrapped his arm around her waist. "Let's see where the evening takes us, shall we?"

"Okay. What first?"

"Let's start with someplace quieter. This way to the docks."

They strolled through the Village and continued toward the docks. They watched a cruise ship depart with the aid of a small tugboat. They waved and smiled as those gathered at the cruise ship's railing called down their last farewells to Key West. "I wonder where they're going next."

"They're probably going to Mexico or to one of the Caribbean islands. That's the usual destination," Dominik said.

"It sounds so incredible. I've never been," she confessed.

"Where, on a cruise or to one of the islands?" he asked.

"Either, neither," she said.

"But I thought you traveled extensively."

"Yes, I do, for my job, and mostly up and down the East Coast. I've never been to the islands and I don't usually take vacations. As a matter of fact, I've never taken a vacation."

"Really?" he said, surprised to hear it.

She nodded. "Really."

"I'd say you were due."

She shook her head. "I don't have time."

"Take the time."

"I have a feeling I could probably say the same of you."

He smiled and chuckled. "Okay, you have me there. No, I don't take vacations as often as some, but I do get away from time to time. My family has a small place out there." He pointed west into the sea.

She looked out at the darkness. "Out where, in the middle of the Gulf of Mexico?" she joked.

"Yeah, as a matter of fact, it is. We have a small island. It's got a cabin that's more like a tree house, but has every imaginable amenity. It even has its own electricity. It's like an upgraded paradise."

"Your family owns an island?"

He nodded. "Yep, 'fraid so," he said.

"Why am I not surprised?"

He pulled her into his arms and kissed her sweetly. "Maybe you'll consider going over with me sometime."

"Yeah, maybe," she said, liking the sound of the invitation and the feel of his arms around her even more.

"Uh-oh, I think our luck's about to run out. I just felt a drop of rain on my arm."

Dominik looked up. There were dark clouds above. "You ready to head back?"

"No, not yet," she said.

"Good." They lingered awhile longer looking out at the dark water without speaking. After a while they headed back to the Village area where the lively street festivals were still going on.

Shauna looked around in awe at the huge differences in the area she once called home. "Wow, I can't believe how different all this looks. It's amazing."

"Yes, there have been major changes in this area of the city, actually in most areas. A couple of bad hurricanes came through and messed up the island pretty badly. A lot of people left and didn't come back. Those who did came back with a renewed vision of a better, stronger city. That vision has resonated and stayed. The city's trying to change a lot of the notions from the past. I think they're doing a good job."

"They are. This area looks wonderful, magical, like a dream," she said. "And I can't believe it's the same place. All the nightclubs and partying. It's so different."

"Yep, Key West is now the place to be to party, which is why the E.R. is always thriving."

"I can imagine."

"It comes in waves. We're just finishing up spring break and now we're into the beginning of the pre-summer season of cruise ships and vacationers. And of course there's always an event or celebration going on here. There are a couple of festivals every month."

He took her hand and guided her across the street. When they reached the other side, he protectively placed his hand at the base of her back. While walking down the street, he pulled her close and whispered in her ear, "Did I tell you how beautiful you look this evening?"

She smiled to herself and blushed. She'd chosen to wear a colorful body-hugging halter dress that flared at the hips. It was definitely sexy and flirty. She'd bought it and never wore it. "No, you didn't."

"Then I have been sorely remiss. You look stunning."

"Thank you."

"You didn't grow up here or we would have met a long time ago. What brought your family here?"

"That's a long, crazy, twisted story."

"We have a long walk back to the car, so it looks like we have plenty of time."

She shook her head. This was something she never talked about to anyone. It was painful. She stopped and looked in one of the storefront windows as they passed. It was an antiques shop. There were dozens of old-fashioned trinkets. She looked each one over as she tried to decide what to say to him.

"Come on, let's go inside," Dominik said.

She looked around at the packed shelves full of antiques and collectibles jammed together. Cluttered and crowed, there were a thousand things to see with absolutely no order. Everything sat next to everything else. Irons, clocks, pots, records, books, small statues, coins, jewelry were all lined up to be viewed. She passed an old typewriter and couldn't help pressing a few keys and shifting over the return lever.

She continued walking to the end of the row and found several stacks of books. She picked up a book, read the title and then skimmed the inside.

"Look at this," Dominik said, pointing to coins in a glass case.

She walked over. "Wow, gold. I wonder if it's real."

"Oh, it's very real," the owner said. "Most of these silver and gold coins come from the *Santa Margarita*.

And yes, I know it sounds like a drink, but actually it's a Spanish galleon. In 1622 it and its convoy sank to the bottom of the Gulf during a hurricane. All hands were lost and millions of dollars in gold, silver and other treasures went with it. All lost to the deep blue sea. That is, until treasure hunting began. We have excursions weekly. You should come."

Another customer asked the owner a question. Dominik stayed with the coins and talked with the owner again and Shauna went back to the books. She continued picking up books and flipping pages. One book she found very interesting. She read more and decided to purchase it.

Dominik was standing outside, waiting.

"Hi," he said. "Looks like you found something interesting."

She looked down at the small bag he carried. "You, too. So, what did you get?"

"I'll show you later. You were right," he said, holding his palm up, "rain." She looked up as she stepped outside. She heard thunder in the distance. Her eyes widened. "We're close to the car. I'll go get it and come back to you."

"No, we can go together. I'll be fine."

"Okay. Come on, we'll be there in a few minutes."

Just as the car was in sight, the clouds burst and rain fell fast and steady. They ran the rest of the way. Dominik opened her car door and she quickly slipped in. He looked at her cautiously. "Are you okay?"

She swallowed hard and nodded. "Yeah, I'm fine. I'm wet, again. It seems like every time I'm around you, I get wet."

He turned, smiling at her, shaking his head. "Woman, do you have any idea what you just said to me?"

"Just drive the car, man," she said, smiling at him, too.

"I'll have you back at the hotel in a few minutes." He started the engine and turned on the windshield wipers.

"Actually," she said, reaching over and placing her hand on his just as he shifted the gear into Reverse, "I'd like to go to your place, if that's okay. I don't feel like being alone right now."

"That's more than okay." They drove to his home in silence, except for the constant patter of rain on the hood. As soon as he parked the car, he looked over at her. "I don't have an umbrella in this car. Here, you can put my jacket over your head."

She scoffed. "What do you think I am, a wimp?"

"All right, you ready to get wet again?"

She nodded and smiled as she removed her heels. "I'm more than ready. Let's do it." She got out, closed the car door, squealed and then ran. "Come on, slowpoke," she hollered over her shoulder.

Dominik laughed and followed. They got to the front door at almost the same time. He quickly opened it and they rushed inside. Breathless and wet, they leaned back against the door, laughing. He held on to her. She wrapped her arms around herself. Her dress was saturated, clinging to her body.

"You must have been a track star in high school or college. Few people can outrun me. You're pretty good," he said.

"Thanks," she said, shuddering. "It's freezing in here."

He draped his jacket over her shoulders. "I left the central-air system on. I guess I'm used to the temperature being cooler. It's a hospital thing."

"Yeah, well, your hospital thing has me shivering."

"Come on upstairs. You can dry off. I'm sure I can find something for you to change into." They went into one of the bedrooms and he continued into the next room. She walked over to the bed. He came back with a towel. Looking at her full body made his jaw drop. The expression on his face was priceless. "The bathroom is in there," he said, heading to the walk-in closet. "Here's a T-shirt and some sweats. I'll get your dress later and send it through the steam dryer. Would you like a cup of hot tea?"

"Oh, yes, that sounds perfect."

Dominik left and Shauna went into the bathroom and grabbed another plush towel from the shelf. She looked at her reflection in the mirror. Her face and hair were wet. She dabbed her face and then removed the clip and dried her hair as she walked back out, looking around the bedroom. She walked over to the bed in the center of the room and pressed down on the mattress. It was big and firm. She wondered what it would feel like to be naked beneath the covers with him.

She reached back to untie her halter dress only to find the knot was wet and had tightened. It was impossible for her to unknot. She twisted it a few times but was only making it worse. She wrapped the towel around her shoulders. She slipped her heels back on. She walked over to the dresser and picked up a bottle of Dominik's cologne. She closed her eyes and smelled it. This was the scent she'd grown to love.

There was a light knock on the door. "Come in," she said.

Dominik opened the door and came inside carrying two cups of tea on a small tray. "I ran out and got these," he said, holding their bags from the antiques store.

"I almost forgot about this." She walked over and took her bag, opened it and pulled out the tissue-wrapped package and handed it to him. "For you."

He was surprised. "What's this?"

"Open it."

He ripped the tissue paper and saw the book inside. He read the cover. "*Medicine, Handbook of Home Medicine* by Dr. R. M. Russell. First edition, copyright 1900. Wow, thank you. This is awesome," he said, already excitedly flipping through the pages. "Some of these remedies are outrageous," he said, chuckling. Then he put it down and grabbed his bag. He pulled out a small box and handed it to her. "For you."

She opened it and beamed. "It's beautiful, but it's too much." She pulled out a gold locket on a gold chain.

"Open it."

She did. There was a small compass inside and the arrow pointed to Dominik. She smiled, then read the inscription—*Points to your true love.* "How did you get it to do that?" she asked. He shrugged and smiled. "It's beautiful, Dominik, but I can't accept it."

"You'll have to. I can't return it to the Santa Margarita."

She smiled. "Thank you. Can you help me put it on?" She gave him the locket and turned around. He put it on her. She smiled, turned and mouthed *Thank you.* He nodded.

"You didn't change?" he queried.

"I couldn't get my tie unknotted. Would you give me a hand?" she said, moving to the mirror.

"Sure." He walked over as she turned to face the dresser and moved her wet hair aside. He pulled a few times, then finally got the wet tie undone. He let the two ends rest on her back.

"Thank you," she said to his reflection without turning around.

"Do you need help with the zipper, too?" he asked her reflection. She nodded. He pulled the small tab down slowly. Her dress loosened around her hips. He rubbed her arms, then reached up to her shoulders and began massaging them. They stared at each other in the mirror.

Shauna closed her eyes and moaned as his hands continued rubbing her shoulders. "Mmm, that feels amazing."

"I'm very good at massages," he said.

"Really? Show me," she coaxed.

"I start here." He began slowly circling her temples with his fingers, then he eased down to her neck and pressed his thumbs to the nape. It was just the perfect amount of pressure. Her shoulders slumped and dropped as his hands rubbed and massaged them. He leaned in and kissed the back of her neck down to her shoulders. He loosened the dress on her hips and let it fall to the floor. She stood topless in the mirror's reflection. He continued massaging her shoulders, then her arms and her hands. He rubbed her neck down to her hips. Then he roamed down her back and around to her breasts.

He encircled and tantalized each already-hardened nipple with his thumb and forefingers. His hands delved down her stomach to rest between her legs. She gasped, remembering what happened last time. She wanted more. She was ready and she wanted all of him. She turned around. He looked into her eyes. His gaze speared her. "I can take you back to the hotel," he said softly.

She nodded her head. "Okay," she said. He nodded and turned to leave. She grabbed his hand and held him still. "Tomorrow," she added with a sly, sexy smile. She reached up and cupped his face. "I need to stay here tonight." She kissed him tenderly, then leaned back. She licked her lips, tasting his sweetness. His tongue slipped into her mouth and she welcomed him completely. She wrapped her arms around his neck and pressed her body closer, feeling the steel hardness of his erection ready for her.

Long, slow, luscious kisses lingered on and on, then turned hungry and ravishing. Each frantic and desperate to connect and hold on as long as possible, as if breaking the kiss would end the world as they knew it. Suddenly, the kisses slowed to tender nibbles again. She slowly pulled his shirt from his pants, then over his head and dropped it with her dress.

She stroked the side of his face, then smiled and walked over to the bed. He watched the gentle spread of her pink lace panties. All he could think about was eating them off her body. He licked his lips in anticipation.

After she climbed onto to the bed, she turned and motioned for him to come to her. Without hesitation he walked over. His eyes focused on every curve of her body. Her breasts, pert and inviting, beckoned to him. There was no need for more foreplay after that. Raw, abandoned hunger took over. The kiss erupted instantaneously. As soon as he reached her, he opened his mouth and took her nipple in. He suckled hard. She gasped and held on tight to his shoulders as his mouth and tongue tickled her body. She quivered and arched her back as he held her tight, cupped her butt and pressed her to his hardness.

She raked her lower lip with her teeth and her hands trembled as she pulled down his zipper. His pants fell to the floor. She reached into his boxers and grasped his rock-hard penis. The feel of his long shaft excited her. She pulled his boxers down and freed him. He stood completely erect. "Condoms?" she said, huskily breathing hard.

"Yeah," he said, reaching down and opening the nightstand's top drawer. He pulled out a small packet and ripped the foil top with his teeth. Shauna smiled with excitement. She took the condom and quickly covered him. He tipped her chin up to see her eyes. They stared at each other for a brief moment. She pointed her finger into his chest, guiding him to lay back. He did. She climbed on top of him and slipped her hand between their bodies. She positioned his penis at the entrance of her core and eased down. He filled her and her body burned with pleasure. He was thick and long and she felt every inch of him entering her. She was tight.

This was her fantasy from as far back as she could remember. She wanted this. She wanted him. And now she had him. She rose up and released him, then sat, filling herself again. He held her hips and she gyrated front to back, building the friction of rapture. She wanted all of him. Breathlessly she pounded onto him and he met her force with equal vigor. Her heart thundered riotously. Every nerve ending in her body quivered.

She thrust hard. He rocked his hips upward to meet her. With her mouth open, she gasped, feeling her climax coming closer and closer. The force of this power was beyond anything she's ever felt. Her body tightened and she shivered as each thrusting surge increased the intensity.

She gasped loudly, holding her breath. Her nails bit into his shoulders as she arched back, reaching and holding on to his thighs. He pumped up and each time she squealed louder and louder. He grabbed her hips and stilled her body, then he increased his thrusting movements. She nearly exploded. She was going mad. Her thighs tightened around his hips.

Winded, she opened her eyes and looked down. He was looking up at her. Her insides melted. He pressed her hips forward, she leaned into him, then he pivoted and turned. She rolled over onto her back. Her legs tightened around his waist. Without missing a beat or breaking their connection, he was now on top. Face-to-face, eye to eye they made love, climaxing together. Their bodies shook as a mighty orgasm ripped through them. Spasms jerked, making them quiver in each other's arms.

She was just catching her breath when he grabbed her butt and raised her higher, then pulled her up to face him. She sat straddling his hips. She wrapped her arms around his neck and he held tight to her waist. He moved his body, drawing a renewed friction, hitting the tiny nub once more. Her body instantly responded. He stared into her eyes. She knew he was making her come again. She couldn't stop it even if she wanted to.

A few seconds later her body tensed and her legs tightened. She gasped, then shrieked as her climax spiked and ecstasy washed over her again and again. She screamed his name. When he finally stopped, she was drained and weak. She couldn't move. She laid her head on his shoulder and he cradled her in his mighty arms.

"I've been waiting a long time to make love to you," he said. She barely heard his words. Her mind had drifted a million miles away.

"Yes. Yes. Yes."

Chapter 14

Shauna slowly opened her eyes as the bright sunshine washed the bedroom with brilliant light. She took a deep breath and snuggled back, feeling Dominik's body pressed close against her. He had his arm draped over her body and around her waist. As soon as she stirred, he wrapped his arm tighter around her and began seductively stroking the side of her body and circling her nipple with his fingers. She smiled to herself. All this man had to do was touch her and she melted.

"Good morning," she said.

"Good morning," he greeted. "How are you feeling?"

She took a deep breath and released it slowly. "I feel fantastic," she said, leisurely stretching and rolling over to lie on her stomach.

"Hmm, yes, you do feel fantastic and the view ain't bad, either," he said as he peeled the covers back to get a better look at her naked body. He began massaging her back and butt. "You have an absolutely stunning rear end." He leaned down and kissed her cheek and caressed her thighs.

"Is that your professional opinion, Doctor?"

"That is most definitely my professional opinion. Your gluteus maximus muscles are perfection. As a matter of fact, I'm seriously considering writing a paper on your rear end and having it published in the *New England Journal of Medicine*."

She laughed. "Thanks, but no thanks. I'd rather not have the entire medical profession checking out my butt."

"As you like, but definitely the journal's loss," he said, kissing the other cheek.

"I think I forgot to tell you that I had an incredible time last night. Thank you for a wonderful evening. I haven't been out on a date in a very long time and never like last night. I guess my next date is gonna be hard to top this one."

"Your next date? Who says this date is over with yet?" he asked, nibbling her back. She giggled. "I have the morning and afternoon off and a whole drawerful of condoms. I suggest we get started right now." He deepened his voice and whispered in her ear. He started kissing her neck.

She rolled over to face him and looked down the length of his body. He was already hard and ready for her. She rolled back over, opened the drawer and pulled out a small foil packet. As she pulled and rolled back over, several connected condoms trailed. She held up ten in total.

"Now, that's what I'm talking about, exuberance and a woman who is assertive." She chuckled. "What?" he asked, smiling.

She shook her head. "Nothing, it's just the Pennington sisters gave me a book called *Dominatrix 101*. Curiously, I flipped through and read the part about being assertive in bed. It was very enlightening."

"Oh, so you want to be a domme now, huh? I guess that means you're gonna need a personal sub."

"Wait, what do you know about dommes and submissives?"

"I'm an E.R. doctor. I've seen just about everything in one form or another over the years. Believe me, there are some positions and situations the unlearned and untrained should not attempt without strong lube and a definite exit strategy."

They laughed. They laid face-to-face staring at each other. She swallowed hard. "I fantasized about being here with you."

He half smiled. "I dreamed about you."

They didn't speak again for a few minutes. She reached out and touched his face. "So many times I wanted to just reach out and touch you, but I couldn't."

He took her hand and kissed her palm. "You're here now."

She nodded. "Two weeks."

He frowned. "That's not enough time."

She smiled, touched by his words. "We both know what this is."

He took a deep breath. "Yeah," he said as he kissed her hand again. "I remember you," he said softly.

"What?"

"From high school, I remember you, quiet, unassuming, shy. I was a senior and you were a junior. You were in my sister's class. I think you purposely tried to fade into the background."

"Yeah, I guess I did. That was me, wallpaper."

"You were only there for junior and senior year. You didn't even go to your prom or graduation. What happened after that? Where did you go?"

"You heard the stories."

"About your father?" he asked, then nodded.

She nodded slowly, then looked away. "Yes. He embezzled money from his job and ran away with another woman. He got caught and he went to prison. My mom and I had to pick up the pieces. The house, the cars, everything was gone. When the kids at school found out what happened…"

"Let me guess, you were humiliated," he surmised. "You didn't do anything. Your father did."

"Yeah, but you know high school. It didn't matter. I wasn't one of the cool kids, so it was easier to just fade into the background and let everything I dreamed about disappear."

"What did you dream about?"

"You," she said, looking at him.

He smiled and nodded. "Tell me about your mother. She died at Key West Medical Center, right?"

She frowned. "I'm not sure how you knew that, but yes, my mother died there. She died the week before I graduated. I took her to the E.R. for help with a bad pain in her head and stomach. I remember it like it was yesterday. It was a bad night. There was a huge storm with rain, lightning and thunder. The winds nearly swept us off our feet, but I got her there. I just knew they would help her. I was wrong. She never came out."

"Did the doctors tell you what happened?"

"Only that she died. We waited in the E.R. for hours. No one would help her because her illness wasn't severe enough. They gave her some kind of antacid prescription and sent her home. I brought her back an hour later. She died waiting."

"That should never have happened."

"No, and now I make sure it doesn't."

He nodded, recognizing she didn't want to go any further. Just then, his cell phone rang. He frowned. "Give me a minute," he said, then got up and grabbed his cell phone from the dresser. He began discussing a medical case with someone.

Shauna got up and went into the bathroom. There was a toothbrush, comb, brush, washcloth and towel on the counter. She closed the door and turned on the shower. There were two separate showerheads, one in front at the top like a sprinkling waterfall and one at the back. She turned them both on. After brushing her teeth, she stepped into the shower and let the warm water pour down the front and back of her body. She just stayed like that for a while thinking about the past few weeks. Being in Key West made her think about the past too much. She poured shower gel on the washcloth and began lathering. She stepped back under the streams of pulsating water, then felt a rush of cool air.

She turned as Dominik stepped in behind her. His eyes were focused and hungry. He went to her and kissed her hard, sealing her body against the shower tiles. The kiss was insane for both of them. They pressed and pushed and grabbed and caressed. Feeding off each other's appetite, they were insatiable in their need.

He dragged his mouth down her body, kissing, licking and suckling her breasts as he stroked the rest of her. He dipped down farther, putting her leg on his shoulder, and ate until she screamed his name again. Quivering and breathless, she dug her nails into his back and shoulders.

Still wanting more, they were fervent and frantic in intent. They both needed this release. It was passion and power gone amok. She pushed him back against the opposite wall and began kissing his body. She dropped to her knees and opened to him.

His long, hard penis stood out at her. He pressed a condom he'd been holding into her hand. She ripped it open and covered him. He picked her up. She wrapped her legs around his waist. She held tight to the nape of his neck as he entered her in one thrust. Her body tensed, then he began moving up into her. The water poured down over them. He thrust in and out over and over again. She held on tight, taking every inch of him.

She felt her body tense again. She held on tighter. He pushed faster, harder, and she demanded more and more. Then in a brilliant blast of red-hot rapture, they climaxed. Jerking spasms shot through them as he held her still and the streams of warm water flowed around them. They stayed like that awhile, neither moving nor wanting to move. Then he released and slowly eased her up to stand on the tile floor. But they still held on tight to each other.

An hour later they lay on the bed, eating breakfast, drinking tea and reading the newspaper. He peeked over his newspaper. "I like this."

"What?" she asked.

"Lying naked in bed with you on a Saturday morning," he said.

"You do, huh?" she said. He nodded. "Well, you can't get too used to this. You know this date is gonna have to end sometime."

"Not necessarily. It can go on for as long as we want."

"Reality check, I'll be leaving your fair city in two weeks."

"Two weeks," he said. "So soon."

She nodded. "It may be even sooner than that. I finished the first two boxes and looked through the others. It shouldn't take long to do them. The first two were the most detailed. I'll have everything I need to make a determination soon."

"And when it's done, then what?"

"I move on to the next job."

"Which is where?"

"I don't know. I haven't decided yet. I have two large clients—Relso Health Care and the Cura Medical Group. Cura wants me to check out a few centers on the West Coast. They're thinking of expanding and want my input. But I'm not sure I want to go west for seven weeks. Plus, the constant traveling is getting tiresome. I have a condo in Maryland, but I haven't been home in over a month."

"You can always turn them both down and stay here."

"My job is on the road."

"Change jobs," he said simply. "You obviously know a tremendous amount about the operation and management of hospitals, clinics and medical centers. Your knowledge and experience are invaluable. You can get a job helping in any hospital or medical center. Imagine turning one of them around from the inside."

"I thought about it and I've been offered a number of very nice positions, but I've never accepted."

"Think about it. Maybe it's time to come home to stay."

"Home is where the heart is," she said, reciting the platitude.

"Where is your heart now, Shauna?"

She smiled. "Right now, it's here with you." She

wanted to say more. She wanted to tell him that her silly high school crush was love and always had been. That every man she ever dated paled in comparison to her dream of him. And that now that dream paled to him. "Want to know a secret?" she asked. He nodded. "I had a huge crush on you in high school."

"I guess that makes us even," he said.

"How so?" she questioned.

"I have a crush on you right now."

She blushed and right then, she felt the love she'd always wanted from him. Whether it was real or just for the moment didn't matter. Right now she was with Dominik Coles and she was loved. "I still want to see that sunset you said was so phenomenal from up here."

He smiled. "Yes, I did, didn't I? I promise you will see the sunset and much more."

"Careful, I might get too used to hanging around."

"Want to hear a secret?" he asked, just like she had moments ago. She nodded. "That's the whole idea."

Shauna didn't respond. She just smiled and went back to reading her newspaper article, although she had no idea what it was about. She read and reread the same sentence over and over again but couldn't discern the meaning if her life depended on it. Her mind was too wrapped up in doing what she wasn't supposed to be doing—feeling. She'd vowed she could take the emotion out of this physical attraction. She knew it was impossible when she agreed.

She had been in love with Dominik Coles the moment

she spotted him in the eleventh grade. Nothing had ever changed. She'd had boyfriends and brief relationships, but there was always Dominik in her heart. Nothing changed. Nothing ever would.

Chapter 15

The next week went by almost as fast as their first weekend together. They worked and did their jobs, but every free second they found they spent together. They watched movies, ate romantic dinners, went dancing and even took a boat out to Cutter Island, his family's vacation getaway just twenty miles away from Key West. It was six and a half miles of pure paradise and Shauna was amazed at how beautiful the island was. And the fact that Dominik's family actually owned it was totally incredible.

They left early from work midweek, grabbed a picnic dinner from Nikita's Café and headed out to Cutter Island. They stayed all afternoon swimming in the waterfall pond, walking, running and playing on the beach, sunning out on the tree-house deck and making love in the sweet grass beside the stream. When evening came, they lay out in a huge, freestanding hammock beneath the stars in each other's arms and witnessed the awesome beauty of the heavens above. A billion stars shone down on them. "This is paradise," Shauna said, snuggling close beside Dominik with just a colorful scarf draped around her hips.

"Now that you're here, it is. I can't imagine spending my nights any other way except with you in my arms," Dominik said as he stroked her arm and kissed her forehead.

"You really need to stop saying stuff like that. It's going to be hard enough leaving here next week." She felt his body tense.

"Don't go," he said.

"I have to."

"No, you don't. Stay here with me." He turned to face her. "I love you, Shauna. Marry me and stay with me," he said softly.

"Dominik," she said, quickly standing up and walking away from him, "please don't do this to me."

"Do what?" he asked, standing up, too. "Shauna, I love you and I know you love me. You can't deny that any more than I can. We can get married right now if you want. I'll set the GPS on the boat. Pick an island— Jamaica, Saint Kitts, St. Maarten, St. Lucia or Antigua. We'll stay a few days, get our license and then marry."

Her heart thundered as her mind scattered in a million different directions. For so long she had wanted to hear those words come from his mouth. She was near tears and breathless at the wishful excitement of it all. But… "Dominik, please, I do love you, so much and for so long I can't even say. But this is my fantasy. How can you possibly be certain you love me after just two weeks together?"

"First of all, this isn't just your fantasy—this is our fantasy. And second, a few weeks, a few days or a few hours, sometimes that's all it takes to start a lifetime together. My cousin told me that a few days ago. And you know what? He's right—time doesn't matter when it comes to love. I love you, Shauna, and you and I will be married, of that I am certain."

She wrapped her arms around his neck and kissed him as tears fell down her cheeks. She was so deliriously happy that she couldn't speak. Maybe, just maybe she'd have that fantasy after all. And if not, at least this was her fantasy for right now. They made love again. This time it was slow and sensual. This was by far the most incredible day of her life.

The next day, Shauna didn't seen Dominik all morning. She assumed as usual he was busy in meetings and in the E.R. They'd always kept their distance at work even though she was sure they weren't fooling anyone.

She called Pearl, who was still away. Shauna had been trying to get in touch with her for the past few days, but her cell phone's message kept coming on and all text messages bounced and failed. She was starting to get concerned when Pearl finally returned her call. "Pearl, hey, how are you?" Shauna asked, relieved to hear her voice. "I was really starting to get worried about you."

"Hi, I'm hanging in there. My friend had a little bit of a relapse and I decided to stay awhile longer. I'm sorry we haven't spent more time together."

"No problem, I'll make sure to come back to visit more."

"How's work going?" Pearl asked.

"Actually, I'm almost done. I just have a few more things to wrap up. I hope I'm gonna see you before I leave."

"Yes, of course you will. I'm on my way home right now. How about us having dinner tomorrow evening?"

"Yes, that's sounds terrific."

"Perfect. I'll call Mae and Wanda and see if they're available to join us."

"That sounds great," Shauna said.

"And maybe you can get the good doctor to come, as well."

"I don't know about that. He may have to work. As head of the department, his hours are always unpredictable."

"Well, ask anyway, just in case."

"Yes, I will."

"And speaking of the good doctor, how is he?"

Shauna smiled to herself. "He's great, amazing, actually."

"Great, amazing. Wow, it sounds like you two got to know each other just a little."

"Maybe a bit more than just a little," Shauna said.

"Does he make you happy?"

"Yes, very much," Shauna said.

"Shauna…"

"Pearl, I know what you're gonna say. Yes, I do love him. I always have. I don't know, maybe I always will. But being with him these last two weeks has been a dream come true for me. I wish what we have right now could last forever, but it can't, and I can be happy with fond memories."

"No, you can't. Sweetheart, I told myself the same thing years ago. I was wrong and I'm not going to lie to you or have you lie to yourself. I can't have you think that the memory of love will suffice, because it won't. You need more. You deserve more," Pearl said, then took a deep breath and exhaled slowly. "But we'll talk when I get home later. I'll call you."

"Okay," Shauna said. "Pearl, are you okay? You sound tired."

"It's been a long week and a half. I'll be fine as soon as I get home. We'll talk then."

"Okay, see you tomorrow night."

Just as she ended her call, there was a knock on the conference room door. "Come in," she called out.

The door opened and Dominik looked in. "May I come in?"

She smiled. "Sure."

He closed the door behind him and walked straight to her. She stood smiling. He wrapped his arms around her waist and kissed her long and lovingly. "Mmm, that was good," he said. "I've been waiting to do that all day."

She giggled as he caressed her rear. "I saw you in the cafeteria earlier. You had the look in your eyes. If anyone saw the way you were looking at me from across the room…"

"What look?" he asked, still leering.

She smiled at the hunger still in his eyes. "That look."

"Oh, you mean this look." He kissed her again. "I can't wait to get you home tonight," he whispered close to her ear, then nibbled her lobe.

"Oh," she said, leaning back but still interested.

He nodded and raked his lower lip with his teeth. "Oh, yeah."

"What do you have planned?"

"A romantic dinner and then strip poker," he said. "You won the last game and I want a rematch. So, what time are you gonna be ready?"

"If I remember correctly, we both won that game. But actually, I'm gonna stay a little later tonight to finish up a couple of things."

"Okay. I'm on my way to Margaret's office. I'll see you later. Clothing is optional."

She laughed. "Go, leave. I have work to do." He turned to go. "Oh, wait," she called to him. He turned, smiling.

"Want to play now? I'm sure I can find a deck of cards."

"You are so bad. No, but I spoke to Pearl earlier and she asked if you'd like to join us for dinner tomorrow night. The Pennington sisters will be there, as well."

"Yeah, I would. That sounds great."

She nodded. "Thanks. I'll tell her and text you the address."

"Okay, see you later."

Shauna watched him go and wondered what she was going to do when it was her turn to walk away. Her plans were set. She was leaving in three days. One last weekend was all she had left.

Dominik headed to Margaret's office. He was walking on air. Everything was perfect. He waved at the receptionist as he headed back to the administrative offices. He knocked on Dr. Gilman's door and waited. She called out for him to enter a few seconds later. "Hi, Margaret. You wanted to see me?"

"Dominik, come on in and have a seat."

He sat down. "So, what's going on?"

"Two things. One, I recently heard from a contact of mine at the Cura Medical Group. Apparently the review being done here isn't showing in our favor. Shauna Banks has discussed some preliminary findings with her associate, Simon Patterson. At this point, with this knowledge, we're assuming the Cura Group will pass on making an offer to purchase this facility," she said.

Dominik nodded his understanding. He wasn't surprised by her findings. The medical center had been mismanaged for years. Dr. Bowman was only the tip of the iceberg. And although Margaret, new to her position as director, was steadily cleaning up what had gone on for years, the damage had been done. "I understand."

"As I'm sure you already know, I'm not at all happy about this and neither is the board. We don't have the funds to keep this hospital open long if this deal doesn't go through. If you have any influence on Shauna, like I hear you do, then I suggest you change her mind fast whether you agree with this buyout or not. It needs to happen. This place needs a buyer. We need funding."

"So, if Cura falls through, can the board get another buyer?"

She shook her head. "No, we're in too far and we're on a shoestring budget right now. We don't have time to start this process all over again. We were lucky to so quickly develop a relationship with Cura and have their interest. I can't see that happening again, not in our time frame. More than likely the board of directors will just drag this out to the end and let it go. I'm concerned about this community. There's no other place to go and get good, reliable medical attention."

"I agree. There's no other hospital close by to take over the lead."

"Obviously this is not official, but it's apparent Shauna will not be recommending us and I think it has something to do with her mother's death. It has become blatantly clear that she never wanted Cura to buy this medical center and I believe I just found out why. You were right about her mother's files. And in anticipation of this going south, I have been instructed by the board to file a preemptive report citing emotional and discriminatory practices by Shauna Banks."

"What?" Dominik asked.

"I had no choice. I turned in my findings to the board and they drafted a response. It will hopefully save the hospital by giving us another chance with Cura, and I assume that's still what you want."

Dominik frowned. "Of course I want to save the hospital, but damaging someone's reputation and possibly their career is a huge price to pay. She's right, this facility is a huge risk. If Cura buys it just to resell, that's not going to help us."

"Still, you were right. This is personal for Shauna. It looks like she's deliberately closing us down out of revenge for her mother's death."

"No, I don't believe that."

"Believe it. After her mother died, she filed a wrongful-death suit alleging hospital negligence complicit with her mother's medical care. In other words, she sued us for malpractice."

"Why would she file a malpractice suit?"

"It was alleged in transcripts that her mother came to the E.R., waited several hours, was seen and then sent home. She returned an hour later in more pain than earlier. She waited a few more hours in the E.R., which ultimately aided and accelerated her eventual demise."

"Did she? Were we responsible?" he asked.

"I don't know. It's not for us to say or to speculate now. Neither of us knows what happened that night. Triage could have missed the signs. Also, there could have been a number of equally urgent medical emergencies going on at the time. But the bottom line is, the hospital board reviewed and examined the situation and ruled the hospital and doctors faultless."

"We examined and ruled on ourselves. That's rich," he said sarcastically. "No wonder she sued."

"No judgments. That was a long time ago."

"Not to a young girl about to start her life with the only parent she had left. No wonder she does what she does. She's trying to help the next person sitting in the E.R. waiting to die with help in the next room but unable to get it."

"That's all well and good, but her intent now seems to be closing down this place. That said, we officially informed the Cura Group of her history with this facility. They assured me that they will look into the situation. We didn't see any other alternative."

"What about patient confidentiality?"

"Her mother was our patient. She's dead. It doesn't apply."

Dominik shook his head. "Ethically that's a thin line. We're still betraying a medical confidence for gain—even if that gain is to save the hospital."

"It can't be helped. We're talking about the needs of the many here. Can the doctors' clinic handle this center's closing?"

Dominik shook his head. "No, we can't absorb the area's medical needs. We're already pushed to an over-capacity situation."

"Exactly," she said. "So, imagine this medical center closing."

"There's got to be another way."

"There isn't. It's already done. This facility is the cornerstone of this community. We not only supply jobs and health care, but we also provide peace of mind. Imagine losing that peace of mind in closing the E.R. The implications are immeasurable. We're in a critical condition here. Filing bankruptcy is the next step. No, the Cura Medical Group isn't the best company to buy this place, but they are the only one offering. And right now we're beggars and we can't be choosy." Margaret paused.

Dominik knew this was going to be a major blow to Shauna. Not only did she still blame this medical center for her mother's death, but they were now going to be also responsible for ending her career. Cura was her biggest client. If they showed no faith in her, she could lose everything.

"You said two things. What's the second?" he asked.

"I haven't told anyone what's going on. The board of directors knows, of course, but no one outside of this office. I'm depending on your discretion. I told you because of your close relationship with Shauna," she said. Dominik looked at her curiously.

"To answer the questions you're not asking, no, I don't

know specifics, but there are rumors, and I'd have to be blind not to see how you look at her."

He nodded. "I don't know what the rumors are, but yes, we're together, and if I had my way, it would be permanent."

She nodded. "Far be it from me to tell you what to do in your personal life. That's not my job. And because neither of you are breaking any hospital ethics rules, it's none of my business. But I wanted you to know this was happening and like everything else, it will come out. If being permanent, as you say, is your goal, you perhaps need to consider her motives in all this. The lawsuit was thrown out. Now I wonder if she's come back to finish what she started. Blocking Cura could do just that."

"Whatever her motives, they aren't to close this facility."

"Are you sure? I hope you're right."

Dominik knew in his heart Shauna held no malice toward the hospital. "I have to get back to the E.R. Thanks, Margaret. I appreciate the heads-up." He got up and headed to the office door. Then he turned around. "Margaret, one more thing. Who did she cite in the malpractice suit?"

Margaret sighed heavily. "Harris Bowman."

Dominik nodded and left.

Shauna's cell phone rang. She checked the caller ID. It was her contact, the executive director from the Cura Group. She answered. "This is Shauna Banks."

"Shauna, it's Simon Patterson. We need to talk."

"Yes, we do."

"I read your review, and quite frankly, we're disturbed about the whole situation."

"What do you mean?"

"You compromised this review."

"Excuse me?" she said.

"We understand you have a personal attachment to this medical center. Your mother died there."

"Yes, she did, but it's not at all a personal attachment. I haven't been back here in over fifteen years."

"Still, you should have told us. Now it looks like the process is tainted. There's no way we can justify going in there now. Your judgment in this matter has been compromised."

"My judgment is just fine, Simon. That's ridiculous. I have always done my reviews based on facts presented. I have never allowed my personal feelings to come into my reviews and certainly not this one."

"One of the doctors there seems to think otherwise."

"What do you mean?"

"I mean we have been given an official complaint citing your emotional and discriminatory practices. You've been distracted and you're off the case."

"What? No," she said and even as the words left her mouth, she knew that only one person knew about her mother and he was the same man distracting her.

"I'm sorry. Pending a formal investigation, we're removing you from these proceedings."

"What about the buy? Are you going forward with it?"

"Taking everything into consideration, there's no way. I can't see how we can. We're passing."

"I understand," she said, knowing it was definitely for the best.

"I'll call you in a few days to let you know of our decision regarding the formal investigation of your actions."

"Goodbye, Simon." Shauna just sat there. She was stunned. Dominik had betrayed her and he got exactly what he wanted—Cura out of the picture. Her heart trembled. She couldn't believe he did this to her. But she couldn't think about that right now. Key West Medical was running out of time and she needed to step up quickly.

The facts remained. Key West Medical Center was still struggling and according to her assessment would close within a year's time. She couldn't let that happen. If Cura wouldn't buy it, she knew someone else who was just as interested. The only thing stopping them before was the Cura Group's interest.

She called her contact at Relso Health Care and sent him some information about Key West Medical Center. Unlike the Cura Group, made up of businessmen and lawyers, Relso Health Care was mostly doctors and those in the medical profession. They had a long history of working closely with medical facilities to get them back on their feet and turning a profit.

She knew Relso Health Care was looking for a purchase in the south Florida area. She stayed on the phone for the next hour and a half. She told them everything, even about her mother. To her relief and joy, they were definitely still interested, and with her urging, they wanted to move fast. As soon as Shauna got off the phone, she headed up to Margaret's office to gauge her interest. "Margaret," Shauna said at the open office door. "Do you have a few minutes?"

"Sure, come in. Actually, I'm glad you stopped by. I need to speak with you, too. Come, have a seat."

Shauna went in and had a seat. For the next five minutes she listened to Margaret convey her regret and disappointment. Shauna sat quietly, seething inside. She had spent the past two hours trying to save an institution that had thrown her under the bus. When Margaret finished, Shauna stood and handed her the key to the conference room and a business card.

"What's this?" Margaret asked.

"It's not the Cura Group, but their pockets are just as deep. I also consult for Relso Health Care. They're dedicated professionals and very interested in buying this medical center. I'd call them now if I were you."

Margaret's jaw dropped as she stood up. Shauna walked out of the office.

Chapter 16

Dominik sat out back in the ambulance bay taking a break from a momentary lull in the ordered craziness of the E.R. Earlier they'd had a car accident, an almost-severed finger, two broken arms, a bar fight with bruises and cuts, and a young couple in for food poisoning. The near insanity of the bustle and commotion finally afforded him a much-needed moment to himself. In the stillness of the approaching evening hours, his thoughts wandered. He looked out as the sky slowly tinted to a darker hue.

A sheriff's car pulled up and parked in the reserved space. His cousin Stephen got out of the car and came over. "Man, you look like crap," he said.

"Thanks." Dominik smirked.

"Nah, I'm serious. For real, you look like crap," Stephen repeated as he sat down beside Dominik on the bench.

"Yeah, I know, I heard you the first time. Thanks," he snapped.

"Whoa, what's going on with you?"

"Sorry. What brings you out to this neck of the woods?"

"I had a domestic backup call a few blocks away and thought I'd stop by and see you. Plus, when I left, they didn't look too pleased. I thought I'd hang out in the immediate area just in case something jumped off again."

Dominik shook his head. "I don't know how you do it. Between you and Natalia, you've taken care of most of the lost souls on this island."

"And you've patched them up and healed their broken bones. But looking at you now tells me this is a little deeper than patient drama. So, what's going on with you? How's Shauna?"

Dominik shook his head. "I just spoke with Margaret. It looks like Shauna had a lot more interest in this place than I thought."

"What do you mean?"

"Years ago she sued the medical center."

"Really? And how did that work out?"

"It was a malpractice suit and she lost. Now Margaret and the board are concerned that this was vengeance. That she wants this facility to close down because she thinks we're responsible for her mother's death."

"Hmm," Stephen said, shaking his head, "that doesn't sound right."

"Yeah, I know. I don't believe it. She's not like that. But the bottom line is, Cura will probably pass on the buy."

"But you didn't want them to buy anyway."

"No, I didn't want the Cura Medical Group. I don't trust them. They're in this business for the wrong reason. But after seven months into this, it's too late to start the process up again with a new company. I hoped we had more time, but the writing's on the wall. It's only a matter of time now."

"Still, the revenge thing doesn't sound right," Stephen said.

"The hospital's legal files are closed, but Margaret read the transcripts. The medical center policed themselves and cleared the E.R. and the doctor involved. I'm sure she was furious after it all went down. Her mother was the only parent she had left."

"Okay, I know you told me not to, but I did it anyway. Yes, Shauna lost the malpractice suit with the hospital, but she won the suit filed in civil court. The hospital settled for an undisclosed amount out of court. It was huge back in the day and in the newspapers for weeks—her father's crime, her mother's illness and then her death, and then the huge lawsuit. But as I understand it, the medical center didn't admit any wrongdoing, but a huge amount of money changed hands in her favor."

Dominik shook his head. This was the part of the

story he hadn't heard. "I don't know what all this means, but I know she'd never intentionally close a hospital."

"How do you know?"

"I know it because I love her."

"Yeah, I know you do," Stephen said. "I also know that I've never known you to even utter those words before. It's all over your face, my man." They both smiled in the joy of feeling love and being loved.

"I love her. From the first moment I saw her sitting in the E.R. wearing a baseball cap, I knew she was going to steal my heart. I also knew there was nothing I could do about it."

"You tell her yet?"

"I told her. We went out to Cutter yesterday. I was ready to set the GPS and head out to Antigua or Jamaica."

"Ah, yes, the wedding bells. What stopped you?"

"We made love instead." They both smiled.

"Will she stay?" Stephen asked.

"I don't know. She'll probably be without a job. The board sent an official complaint to the Cura Group about her undisclosed history with the medical center. They probably won't be happy about it."

"How did the board find out about her mother in the first place?"

"I told them. Actually, I told Margaret and she told them along with everything else. They're desperate."

Shauna was on her way out, but needed to make one last stop. She went to Dominik's office. The door was closed. She knocked but there was no answer. She went into the E.R. area. He wasn't there, either. She found Nora Rembrandt, his assistant. "Hi, Nora. Have you seen Dominik?"

"That's funny, he was just looking for you about fifteen minutes ago."

Shauna looked around. "Do you know where he went?"

"No, but if I see him, I'll tell him you're looking for him. Where are you gonna be?"

"Don't worry about it, I'm headed out."

"If it's an emergency, I can page him," Nora added.

"No, that's okay."

"Oh, wait. Check out back at the ambulance bay."

She exited through the huge extra-wide double doors. She immediately saw two men sitting on a picnic table with their backs to her. She overheard the last part of their conversation. Her heart dropped. She was stunned. Dominik betrayed her and told the board about her mother. She took a deep breath knowing this was the end. "Dominik," she said.

Both men turned around. "Shauna," Dominik said.

"Hi, Shauna," Stephen said, smiling.

She smiled at him. "Hi, Stephen. It's good to see you again."

"You, too. Well, I'd better get back to work. I'll talk to you later. See ya, Shauna."

"It was nice seeing you," she said, then watched as he got in his car, backed up and pulled away. Dominik stood and walked over to her. "I can't believe you told them about my mother. Does the word *confidence* mean nothing to you?"

"Shauna, calm down. It wasn't a secret."

"It was to me. Who did you tell?"

"I told Margaret. She found out the rest and told me."

"My family life was a circus once before. Now my life is private. It was nobody's business about my family and certainly not Margaret's or the board of directors' or the Cura Group, or did you forget to mention you told them, too?"

"You're talking about the complaint to Cura? What happened?"

"What do you think happened?"

"They fired you."

"You never told me how you found out in the first place."

"I was curious, so I looked up your records and then your mother's. Why didn't you tell me the rest of it, the lawsuit? You sued Bowman."

"Yes, as I recently found out, I was the first of many. And you told the Cura Group and got exactly what you wanted. They will not be purchasing the medical center."

"Yes, that is what I wanted. They're nothing but a gang of medical raiders," he said quickly, then turned, hearing the sound of an ambulance in the distance. "The question is, did you get what you wanted?"

"What's that supposed to mean?"

"The medical center is closing."

"And you think I would want this place closed?" she asked.

"No, but a lot of people are going to." Dominik looked up and saw the rage in Shauna's eyes. "Shauna, am I missing something?"

"What could you possibly be missing? And tell me, how could you love a woman if you think she is so bent on revenge that she'd close a hospital, making thousands suffer?"

Just then, an ambulance came barreling up the driveway toward the bay. Dominik's attention was immediately diverted. The doors opened and several attendants gathered beside him. They looked at Dominik and Shauna, but then focused on the ambulance backing up into the bay. Shauna stepped aside, out of the way.

The ambulance's back doors opened and a perfectly performed ballet of chaos ensued. People were yelling, orders were being barked out and everyone was in fast-forward mode. Someone yelled "Flatline" and things got even more chaotic. Dominik was in the center of it all. She watched as everything they were discussing vanished and his focus was on saving the life slipping away on the gurney.

A few minutes later everyone disappeared inside. Shauna was left alone in the bay. She looked around. How could her silly problems compare to the person whose life they were desperately trying to save? This place could never close down. She waited another minute, then headed around to the front of the building.

She was midway to her car when she heard someone calling her. She turned and saw Donna running toward her. "Donna, what is it?"

"You need to come with me now," she said.

Shauna's heart dropped. "What? What is it?"

They started running. As soon as they got inside, Donna swiped her card and led Shauna through to the back. "Wait here," she said, then hurried down the hall to where several doctors, nurses and attendants gathered in one room.

Shauna was anxious. Ten minutes later Donna came back. Shauna stood, then saw Dominik coming toward her quickly. Donna smiled and kept walking. She met Dominik halfway. "What's going on?" she asked. "What happened?"

"Shauna, the person on the gurney is Pearl Tyson."

There was a loud rushing sound as her breath escaped. Her legs trembled and buckled. All she could see was the ceiling as she slowly felt herself falling. Then strong arms caught her. "Shauna. Shauna," Dominik said, moving to sit her back down. "Shauna, listen to me. Pearl is fine."

She nodded. Donna was there with a cup of water. Dominik helped her sip it. Then she caught her breath. The words were finally beginning to make sense. "Pearl," she said.

"Yes, that was Pearl in the ambulance. She has you listed in our files as her next of kin."

"Why is she in your files?"

"She's stable. She just had a small episode."

"A small episode. What are you talking about? Are you kidding me? I saw what happened out there. She flatlined."

"She's fine. I need to get back in to see her. Are you going to be okay?"

She nodded. "Go, take care of her. Please, she's all I have."

He leaned in and kissed her gently. "No, she's not. You have me, always and forever." He walked back to the room. Nora and Donna smiled, as did a few other staff witnessing the kiss.

Chapter 17

Shauna waited by Pearl's bedside in ICU for hours. Then the hours turned into the next day. Pearl had woken up only two or three times since she was admitted. And then she was groggy and incoherent. But Shauna had no intention of leaving her side anytime soon. Several nurses stopped by to tend to her, including Donna, whose reassuring words comforted her. They brought by a few sandwiches and a tray of food, but Shauna couldn't eat.

As time passed, Shauna looked out the window, then watched the respirator go up and down and then tried to figure out what the machine was doing each time it beeped. But mostly she stood vigil. She only left the room when Dominik came in to check on Pearl.

She laid her head down on the side of the bed and

closed her eyes for what seemed like a brief moment.
She dreamed that Pearl was talking to Dominik. He said
that he loved her and that they would be married. Pearl
said that she and her mother had already planned her
wedding. She felt his gentle kiss on her lips and then the
dream was gone. She opened her eyes just as Dominik
walked out of the room. It wasn't a dream, at least not
all of it. He'd been there with her.

"Lord, that is one man in love."

"Pearl, you're awake," Shauna said, hearing her
friend's husky voice. She sat up quickly and looked at
the head of the bed. She smiled giddily when she saw
Pearl's eyes were open, but Pearl was frowning. "What,
are you in pain? I'll call for a nurse." She jumped up.

"No, no, I'm fine. I have enough pain medicine in
me to sedate a herd of elephants. Come back. Sit down."

Shauna walked back over to the bed and looked at
Pearl. "You scared me."

"I scared me," she said.

"The good news is, you're gonna be fine. I still don't
know why you didn't tell me you were sick, but I should
have recognized it as soon as I saw you. You don't eat,
you lost weight and you cut your long hair off."

"Shauna, there's nothing anyone can do. I've been
in remission before and I'll be in remission again. And
you were here to work and hopefully have a little fun,
not babysit me in a hospital room. I had the best care I
could have. Dominik saw to that years ago. I'll be fine."

Shauna shook her head. The sick friend Pearl had

been visiting for the past two weeks was actually her in the hospital getting her chemotherapy treatment. "Do you have any idea how close you came to not being here? You drove home when you should have still been in the hospital. I can't lose you, too," Shauna said with tears in her eyes.

"You won't," Pearl said, then took her hand and squeezed it tenderly. "That's why I need you to find Dominik for me. Fix this. Fix this now."

"Pearl," Shauna said woefully.

"Don't Pearl me. It's been two weeks now and you're both so much in love you don't know what to do with yourselves. Now, I don't know what the problem is, but whatever it is, neither one of you is lying here in this bed, so I'm thinking it's not life-and-death. Whatever happened between you needs to be over. Life's too short for this nonsense. Now, am I gonna have to get up from this bed and get him for you?"

Shauna shook her head.

"Tell me, do you love Dominik?" Pearl demanded.

"Yes, so very much," she said. "I can't imagine my life without him."

"You never have to. I love you now and always."

Shauna turned around to see Dominik standing in the doorway. She stood slowly. Pearl smiled. "Now, would you two please get out of my room and let me get some rest?"

Shauna laughed. "Yes, I think we can do that."

"Come on, I have something for you to see," Dominik said.

Shauna turned and spared one last glance at Pearl smiling. She nodded. "Come back and see me tomorrow."

"I will," Shauna said.

"We will," Dominik said, taking Shauna's hand.

They stopped by his office to lock up as Margaret came walking down the hall, smiling. "Hey, I'm glad I caught up with you two. I have some wonderful news."

"What?" Dominik said.

"Relso Health Care has made an open offer to buy pending a formal review."

"What? How did that happen? I thought we couldn't get another company," Dominik said.

"Shauna made a call after Cura officially pulled out. It looks like Relso Health Care had been shadowing their progress. Cura walked away and Relso stepped right up. It seems like we just might have a deal. But there is one slightly major contingency."

"What?" Shauna asked.

"They want us to immediately hire an operations manager to both oversee the buy and transition and then to keep the medical center on track. I told them I already had someone in mind. Because, of course, once she's married to our permanent E.R. director—congratulations, by the way—she's going to need a new job here in Key West."

"Married?" Shauna said.

Dominik smiled. "I believe a number of hospital staff members are taking bets on our wedding date, the time and the weight of our firstborn. I heard Rodney's taking the bets."

Shauna shook her head.

"Carry on," Margaret said as she quickly walked away after her usual quick wave.

"Married?" she said again.

"Yes, married as soon as humanly possible."

"You know what? I kinda like that idea."

"Me, too," he said and kissed her tenderly. "Come on."

"Now where are we going?"

"You'll see," he said as they waved and walked out. They drove to his house and kept going until they got to his bedroom. He took her hand and walked over to the balcony. He opened the glass door and they stepped outside just as the awesomeness of sunset exploded.

"Oh," she whispered in awe.

"Phenomenal?" he queried. She nodded. "Good." He took her hand and kissed it, placing a beautiful antique ring on her third finger. "Shauna Banks, would you be my wife?"

Tears streamed down her face. "Yes. Yes. Yes." She leaped into his arms and he held her tight. "It's beautiful."

"What, the sunset or the ring?"

"Everything," she said.

"No, you're beautiful. And this is the beginning of

our life together. I love you, Shauna, and I always will. We belong to each other. I'm yours and you are mine."

She took a deep breath and nodded, then reached up and touched his face lovingly. "Yes, mine at last."

* * * * *

Her happiness—and their future—are in his hands.

Essence
Bestselling Author
GWYNNE FORSTER

ECSTASY

ESSENCE BESTSELLING AUTHOR
GWYNNE FORSTER

Teacher Jeannetta Rollins is about to lose something infinitely precious: her eyesight. Only surgeon Mason Fenwick has the skills to perform the delicate operation to remove the tumor that threatens her with permanent blindness. But the brilliant doctor left medicine after a tragedy he could not prevent, and now he is refusing her case. But Jeannetta is nothing if not persistent....

"*Ecstasy* is a profound literary statement about true love's depth and courage, written with elegant sophistication, which is Ms. Forster's inimitable trademark." —*RT Book Reviews*

REQUEST YOUR FREE BOOKS!

2 FREE NOVELS
PLUS 2 FREE GIFTS!

KIMANI™
ROMANCE

Love's ultimate destination!

She's tempted
by a delicious
relationship....

Way to her heart

Melanie Schuster

Sherry Stratton has no time for romance. But every time she's around chef Lucas Van Buren her temperature starts rising! When Sherry finally gives in, the lovemaking is oh-so-sweet. And Lucas thinks they're solid. But when someone from Sherry's past suddenly resurfaces, their delicious relationship is put to the test....

"It is refreshing to finally see an intelligent
heroine with a great backstory."
—*RT Book Reviews* on *Chemistry of Desire*

*Available March 2013
wherever books are sold!*

KPMS2970313